Christmas
IN EVERGREEN
Letters to Santa

Based on the Hallmark Channel Original Movie

NANCY NAIGLE

Print ISBN: 978-1-947892-39-2
eBook ISBN: 978-1-947892-57-6

www.hallmarkpublishing.com
For more about the movie visit:
https://www.hallmarkchannel.com/christmas-in-evergreen-letters-to-santa

Chapter One

Deep in the valleys of Vermont, there's a town called Evergreen. It's said that Evergreen is so far north that on clear days you might be able to see the North Pole. Perhaps that's why townsfolk take Christmas very seriously all year long, even going so far as to have a picture of Santa waving on the "Welcome to Evergreen" sign on the way into town.

The city of Burlington, not so far away, moves at a faster pace. The town bustles with the rush of holiday shoppers carrying their special finds and colorful packages.

At Spruce Collectibles, Lisa Palmer and her business partner, Oliver, were both hard at work. They'd been hired to stage the boutique store for its annual Christmas sale.

Lisa worked the last sparkling blue ribbon from the top of a tall Christmas tree all the way to the bottom. She tucked it deep into the evergreen branches every foot or so, then let it billow down to the next spot, an exercise in precise disarray that made the tree appear full and elegant. It had taken Lisa over fifty yards of wired ribbon to pull off the look, but it was worth it.

She'd adorned the rest of the tree with untraditional blue hydrangea and beautiful glass balls in various shades of blue: royal, sky blue, and even turquoise. Flocked pinecones and fresh chartreuse pears offered a gorgeous contrast against the dark green boughs. At the top of the tree, a brown speckled partridge in a nest of silver lace tied into the store's "Twelve Days of Christmas" theme.

Concentrating on the task at hand, Lisa tucked silver poinsettia picks between the branches to fill any bare spots. She stepped back to evaluate the tree, then turned to Oliver. "Does this line up?" She gestured to the way she'd arranged the poinsettias.

Over his shoulder, the ever-stylish and funny Oliver, wearing a burgundy V-neck cashmere sweater, turned from the display of white candles he was working on to check it out. "Yeah. Perfectly."

"Ugh." She winced and dropped her hands to her side. "Then I have to start over." She plucked four poinsettias from the tree.

"Oh, good," Oliver said facetiously. "I was worried we'd be done in time to get dinner."

Dinner is overrated. He was mocking her. "You know symmetry is just—"

"—lazy design!" they said at the same time.

"Yes, I know." Oliver echoed the sentiment with a smile. He moved one of his symmetrically arranged candles out of position. Their icy evergreen scent lifted into the air like a Christmas hello. Nodding with satisfaction, he spun around and walked toward Lisa. "Note to self, when we open our own store everything's going to have to be just slightly off-kilter." He exaggerated the comment with hand gestures.

"Yes. Impeccably designed," Lisa said with a high-falutin' accent. She handed off a few of the sparkling poinsettias to Oliver to place.

"And locally sourced."

"Uh-huh." She giggled, then tucked another flower into just the right spot on the tree.

It was so nice to work with someone that saw things the way she did. She and Oliver were always finishing each other's sentences, and this job had come together so well she couldn't wait for the store owner, Polly, to see it.

Oliver took one poinsettia from the other side of the tree and repositioned it slightly askew. "The tree really does look great."

She took a giant step back and put her hands on her hips to give it a sweeping up-and-down glance. "Yeah. It does." She folded her arms across her chest with satisfaction.

"Wait." Oliver looked past her toward the back of the store. "Do you think we need a second tree back there?"

She glanced over her shoulder, then spun to his side. "You know what? I was just thinking that." She

Nancy Naigle

gestured toward the back of the store. "I mean, it would pull the eye of the customer back that way—"

Oliver said, "—and that's where the most expensive items are."

"We need a—"

"—second tree," they finished the sentence together again.

"Yeah." She tapped her fingers beneath her chin. Slightly squinting, she imagined how it might look nestled between the beautiful maple shelving units. A second tree would be perfect, but if Polly was happy with what they'd done, she'd have to let it go. The Christmas decorations had been an added "thank you" for the big contract they'd completed for her. Anything else would just cut into their profit.

A knock at the door broke her focus on the back of the store. Lisa spun around to look. "Oh! There's Polly."

The store owner stood waving from the sidewalk. Bundled in a camel-colored wool cape, she looked like she was bubbling over with excitement. Lisa felt excited herself to flaunt all the hard work they'd completed. She patted Oliver on the arm and dashed over to open the door.

"Hi. Come on in."

"Hello!" Polly didn't waste a moment rushing into the store to see what changes they'd made. She didn't even bother to put down her purse and gloves. After taking one glance, she gasped. "It looks amazing in here! Oh my gosh." She waved an arm where the register counter used to be.

"Yeah, we moved the counter to the side of the store—" Oliver started.

"Which opens up the flow from the door to the rest of the store," Lisa finished. They simultaneously gestured to the back of the store as if they'd choreographed the move.

"And you re-designed the entire shelving unit." Polly's head swiveled, taking in all the changes. "It looks great over there."

Lisa and Oliver shared an appreciative glance. Thank goodness Polly was happy with what they'd done. It was a significant change.

Polly moved through the store, zigging and zagging as things caught her eye, and then made a beeline for the tree Lisa and Oliver just finished decorating in the center. "And to top it all off, you decorated for Christmas!" She walked around the tree, slowly examining the different ornaments, still clutching her red gloves in her hand. She oohed and ahhed at the sight of the shiny decorations.

Pointing to the tree topper, she looked perplexed. "Is that a partridge?"

"In a pear tree?" Oliver said with a smile. It had been his idea. "Yes, it is."

Polly beamed.

"And we have two turtle doves." He led her over to the two frosty white-feathered birds next to the candles. "Three French hens." Ceramic ones nestled on

5

a stack of embroidered flour sack towels. "Four calling birds, and five golden rings." He pointed toward the different size rings that now hung above the checkout.

Polly's excited giggle filled the space with even more joy.

"It's just a little service we throw in for jobs this time of year." He looked over at Lisa with a wink and a smile.

"You two are the best at redesigning stores like this. Have you ever thought of opening your own store?"

His face lit up. "In fact, yes," he blurted at the same time Lisa said, "Eventually."

The two of them looked at each other, realizing they'd just given Polly a mixed message.

"Yes." Lisa tried to correct the faux pas.

"Eventually," Oliver added.

"Well, you know I'm expanding, right? I plan to open three new stores in the new year."

"That's great. Where are you thinking?" Oliver asked.

"I'm still searching for locations, but I would love your expertise when designing them, if you're free for more work."

"Of course!" Lisa brightened. "Yes."

"Yes," Oliver agreed.

"We would love to help in any way we can." Lisa bumped Oliver's shoulder with excitement.

"Wonderful." Polly rushed around the store, reveling in every little change. "Goodness. Yes."

Lisa and Oliver shared a silent celebration at the

prospect of working with Polly again. Seeing their clients this delighted was the best part of the job. The only thing left to do was stick around to make sure all the employees knew where everything was located now, and be on standby as the first customers came in for any last-minute adjustments on staging that didn't work out quite as well in real time as it had on paper.

Later that day, Polly signed off on the completed project. Lisa and Oliver headed out of the store together, ready to head their separate ways for the holidays.

Now Oliver would go back to Boston. That was his town, and he loved it. Lisa wasn't entirely sure of her plans since her parents were traveling.

She let out a big sigh as she pulled her leather jacket on over her sweater. "You know if we keep getting work at this rate, we'll be able to open our own store in less than two years." Even though they'd talked about it many times, she wasn't entirely sure how she felt about it now that it was becoming closer to a reality.

"The very best in home decoration and design," Oliver said with pride. "Custom kitchenware, fixtures, and design accessories. Everything you need to turn your house into a...home." Oliver turned to catch up with Lisa, who was double-timing it down the street. "What?"

"Nothing, it's just that..." She sighed again. Heavier this time. Still walking she turned to Oliver. "I love what we do. We get to travel around and redesign spaces."

"I know. I know. We've made it through every business decision, every terrible date."

Lisa thought about the time she had to tell Oliver he wore too much cologne. She loved working with him—bad high-dollar cologne and all. They really could get through anything together. He was her best friend.

"Look." She never broke stride. "All I'm saying is that I'm just not sure that I'm ready to put down roots and stay in one place."

"Ah. And speaking of which…someone has their final New Year's resolution from last year to take care of." Oliver tapped his watch. "Time is ticking."

Lisa groaned.

"Every year we make these resolution lists and every year you have the same goal—"

Lisa rolled her eyes. "Visit my hometown for Christmas. I know. I know. But what if it's not the same as I remember as a kid?" Ruining the picture of the perfect Christmas in her mind was a big risk. Memories of Evergreen had carried her for a lot of years. If she lost that, she didn't know what she'd do.

"Then either way, you'll cross it off your list."

She pursed her lips. "But I was just thinking that maybe I should wait for my parents to go."

"But your parents," Oliver said as he stepped in front of her, "are in Europe. And working. You're not. Now you can go back to your hometown."

She didn't have another valid argument. Honestly, Evergreen was her best memory, not really her parents. They might never want to go back. They'd never even talked about it.

"Let me show you." She pulled her phone up and tapped on it. Stepping closer to him, she brought up her favorite snow picture of Evergreen, taken from the highway overlooking the town below. It was a true winter wonderland.

"Look," she said. Even just looking at photo made her heart happy.

"That's gorgeous."

"Isn't it cute?" She remembered every store on that street, even after all these years.

Oliver, always the voice of reason, said, "Okay, come on. Drive off to this almost real-life Santa's village, take a quick look, and then come back to Boston in time for Christmas Eve dinner."

She cocked her head.

"And by the looks of that town," Oliver went on, "you'll be dressed up as one of Santa's elves and handing out candy canes."

Laughing, she stepped off the sidewalk toward her car. "You know, I think you underestimate how good I would be as one of Santa's helpers." She tossed her hair back as she unlocked the door on her bright green Mazda.

"I don't think I am." He pushed his hands into the pockets of his wool coat. "Now get on the road. Have fun. Enjoy...what's the name of the town again?"

Still holding on to the door with one foot inside her car, she lifted her chin. "Evergreen."

She pulled away from the curb, waving to Oliver. He looked as excited for her as she felt. And now the idea of going back to Evergreen had her stomach full of butterflies, or maybe they were more like swirling snow angels.

Evergreen. Here I come.

Chapter Two

*L*isa navigated the busy city streets of Burlington through holiday traffic to the highway. Utility work had traffic in a snarl, and she was too far in to take an alternate route. It took fifteen minutes to go two miles, making getting out of the city for the holidays even more appealing. Once she got out of the city limits, traffic cleared right up and the snowy mountains looked beautiful. She pressed the radio buttons until she found the Hallmark Sirius XM channel.

Light traffic, clear weather, and good old-fashioned Christmas carols. This drive had all the ingredients for a great road trip. She tapped to the tempo of the music on her steering wheel, singing along when she knew the words.

The curving mountain roads were clear, but snow piled along the sides of the road where the snowplows had done their duty to keep folks safe. The icy trees glistened as perfectly as if she'd done the decorating herself. *Perfectly imperfect.*

The closer she got to Evergreen, the heavier the snow. That added to her happiness. Maybe there would be a snow angel in her future. She hadn't made one since... It had definitely been way too long.

She took the Evergreen exit from the highway, reducing her speed on the quaint country road while still belting out fa-la-la-la-las. Up ahead, a red truck with pine trees in the back stood at the stop sign. She pulled up behind it. After a moment, when the truck hadn't budged, she rolled her window down and peered around it. That's when she realized the hood of the truck was up.

Aw, man. She leaned her head out the window.

"Are you having trouble with your truck?"

"It's not my truck," a man's voice said.

What kind of answer was that? "Is it stolen?"

A dark-haired man with what looked like a day's worth of beard poked his head around the truck.

"No. It's on loan from a friend," he said with a smile. A very attractive smile, Lisa couldn't help but notice.

The truck had to be an early '50s model. Nice. She could've done without the gaudy wreath on the back, but it was a sweet ride. Who loaned that kind of vehicle to someone? They must've been a pretty good friend.

She didn't know why she had the urge to tease

him, but she gave in to it. "Ohhh," she said with an exaggerated moan. "You broke your friend's truck?"

That got a reaction out of the guy. He stepped out from the front of the truck, looking on the defensive. "I didn't break it, it was already…"

Lisa almost grinned, nearly breaking the ruse, then frowned in an attempt to look serious. "Hey, it looks to me like it—"

He shook his wrench in her direction. "You're just messing with me." His smile registered in his eyes as he laughed.

Busted. "I am. I am." She flung open her door and got out. "No. Seriously. Can I do something to help?"

He eyed her cautiously as he wiped his hands on a red shop rag. He was wearing an army green down jacket, and he didn't seem the least bit worried about dirtying the off-white sweater beneath it. "How are you with old engines?"

"Astonishingly good," she admitted. Years of hanging out with her grandfather every summer in his garage while he worked on his old cars had paid off.

The old truck looked to be in great shape. It had either been kept in a garage and treated with white gloves, or there'd been one heck of a restoration on it. The flame-red paint job was so perfect it looked like it had just come off the line. Live pine roping ran from down each side of the front quarter panels, much more alive than the truck at this moment.

He looked unsure whether to believe her. "Really?"

"Yeah. May I?" She took the wrench from his hand,

noticing that his shiny red toolbox was from about the same era as the truck. *Nice.* "Thank you." She leaned in to look under the hood. "All right. What have we got here?" She reached in and gave something a tap. "Have you tried this?"

"Yep."

The motor was clean. Someone took superb care of this ride. The spark plugs didn't appear corroded or oily, but she tapped on the spark plug wire just the same. "How about this?"

"Twice," he said.

"Hmm. I bet you haven't tried this."

But before she could give the battery cable a good jiggle he said, "Yes. I tried that too."

"Ah, but…" Lisa reached in to the engine and cranked the wrench against something that seemed a little stuck. "Let me just…" She got it to budge, then stood back. Handing the wrench to him, she asked, "Do you mind if I try to start it?"

"No, go for it."

"This is a beautiful old truck." She crossed in front of him, opened the driver's door and climbed in.

"Yeah, isn't it?"

She closed the door. On the seat of the truck was a clipboard with an employment application for Banford Logging, Inc., already filled out. The guy's name was Kevin Miller. *He looks like a Kevin.* In the passenger's seat, a wooden crate overflowed with fresh vegetables: collards, sweet potatoes, eggplant, carrots, zucchini and peppers. They made her a little hungry for a good stir-fry. "All right." She leaned forward and twisted the key. The engine struggled.

"Hold on a second," he said.

"Yep." She took her hand from the key and put both of her hands in the air.

He did something under the hood, then stepped out where she could see him. "Okay. Try it again."

She turned the key and the truck started right up.

"Hey! Look at that!" She rested her elbow out the window. "Teamwork."

"Yeah." He walked over to the driver's side of the truck. "Although I contend that I did most of the work, and most of that before you got here." He leaned against the front fender, just behind the cute little round side mirror.

"That is fair. However." She raised a finger toward him. "Had I not come along, you'd still be standing here with your little feet in the snow."

"Also fair." His friendly smile sent a zing right through her that could've melted that snow.

He opened the door for her. "You headed into Evergreen?"

"Am I that obvious?" She stepped out of the truck. "Christmas tourist. Headed into town to see the famous snow globe." She liked the easy banter with him, and she wondered what his story was. If he were a local to Evergreen himself, then he'd know she was just passing through.

"No. You're not that obvious. It was a lucky guess. This is the only road in or out of town."

"Oh. Well, yeah, there's that, huh?"

"There's that." He leaned against the truck door with that drop-dead gorgeous smile.

Was he flirting with her?

"Well, um." She almost didn't want to leave, but she really had nothing else to say.

"Thanks."

"You're welcome," she said. "Merry Christmas."

"Merry Christmas, and all that. Welcome to Evergreen." He slammed the door shut on the truck, but stood there as she walked back to her car.

"Thanks." She was glad he couldn't see the slight blush on her cheeks. She pulled around the truck, giving him a quick double-toot of her horn as she drove by.

Helping a stranger. Now, that was a great way to start a holiday.

Lisa waved as she passed Kevin standing next to the truck at the stop sign. Through the intersection, then just around the bend was the familiar "Welcome to Evergreen" sign. It still carried the picture of Santa on it.

Hello, Evergreen.

Her pulse quickened as she started through the red covered bridge that led to town. As she drove through, the tires echoed a thumpity-thump with each turn over the wooden beams. She used to lift her feet when Daddy drove through it, although back then she'd referred to it as a tunnel. It wasn't nearly as big or long as it had once seemed, either.

Almost there.

A short drive brought to her to Main Street. Evergreen wasn't disappointing her yet. Giant candy canes hung from every lamppost. Christmas trees in all different sizes decorated with shiny ornaments offered a dazzle of color against the snow-laden trees. Every store on the street was ready for the holiday, too. The town was as amped up for the season as she remembered—in a way that could put any other quaint New England town to shame.

She parked in front of the Chris Kringle Kitchen. It looked the same, with the jolly Santa with his bag slung over his shoulder on the sign. What was new were the half-dozen charming wrought iron bistro tables painted in alternating red and white. A young couple sat with their coffee at one of the small tables outside near one of the tall propane heaters.

Lisa got out of the car and tilted her chin to the sky. The fresh scent of pine, mixed with the savory smells of good home cooking, hung in the air.

She turned toward the Chris Kringle Kitchen and then paused, remembering. All those years ago, before they'd moved away, she'd stood right there in the cafe and shook the magical snow globe. She remembered the way the snow swooshed around the church in the glass dome. She'd wished she could stay in Evergreen forever.

Lisa turned and looked across the street. There sat Daisy's Country Store…dark and quiet now. The top of the sign had slipped from its hold, leaving it off-kilter and not in a pretty way. In the door's window, hanging on a string, a sign read, "Sorry, We're Closed." It looked as though it had been that way for a while.

Her mood dipped. Daisy's Country Store had been the heartbeat of this town when she was a little girl.

Lisa lost herself in memories of the last time she'd been there.

In her mind it was the Nineties again. The sky faded to night, snow was falling, and the inside of the store was lit up, ready for customers. Back then, the store had been garnished in pine garland with tiny colorful twinkle lights. Glass balls hung in the storefront windows from shiny ribbons and an illuminated Santa welcomed customers at the front door.

She imagined it as clearly as if she were there right at that moment. The store was alive with the energy of customers, and Daisy herself was puttering around, as delightful as always, with her ever-present smile. Daisy had been dressed like she was ready for Sunday church, wearing sparkling gold jewelry and smelling of peppermint.

Lisa remembered being in the store to write out her final letter to Santa using the colored pencils Daisy kept by Santa's mailbox. She'd been wearing her favorite purple Christmas cardigan that day.

Dear Santa,
This year for Christmas I would like...

Daisy leaned forward on the counter. "Did you put your truest Christmas wish in your letter?"

She wasn't entirely sure. "Maybe." She finished writing and then turned her letter to show Daisy.

Daisy looked surprised. "Are you sure I can read it?"

She'd nodded, secretly hoping maybe Daisy could help her wish come true.

Daisy read the letter. "I would like to have Christmas in Evergreen every year." She held the letter in her hand and then turned it back toward Lisa. "Is that your truest wish?"

Lisa's eyes filled with tears. She didn't want to cry in front of everybody, but she didn't want to leave Evergreen. "We're moving away. And I'm excited. But I love Evergreen, so…"

Daisy patted her hand. "Lisa, what about this? What if instead of saying you'd like to have Christmas *in* Evergreen every year, you'd like to have Christmas *like it is* in Evergreen. That way, wherever you go, you can always feel the warmth of home. Every year."

Lisa recalled the relief Daisy's words had brought her. She had that kind of warmth about her. Always a kind word. Always a note of wisdom in everything she said.

Daisy had picked up a green colored pencil and fixed the letter, then folded it and placed in the fancy red mailbox with a loving tap. Lisa still pictured Daisy's warm smile…she could almost feel its effect on her right now.

There were several people moving about Main Street this morning. Lisa pulled her purse up onto her shoulder and walked toward the Chris Kringle Kitchen.

A woman wearing jeans, a white shirt and a pretty burgundy cardigan placed the specials chalkboard on one of the cafe tables outside of the cafe. According to the sign, today's special was roast beef. A funny reindeer smiled from the bottom of the sign.

"Excuse me," Lisa said, approaching the woman. "Could you tell me what happened to Daisy's store?"

"Oh. Uhm?" The woman gave a thoughtful tilt of her head. "It closed. A little over a year ago."

"That's a shame. I loved that place."

"Truly! It was the anchor of town," the woman said. "Made of joy, that place."

"Yeah." That was exactly the way she remembered it, too. She felt almost afraid to ask, but she did, anyway. "And Daisy?"

The woman's eyes filled with sorrow. "Daisy... passed away this year."

"Oh." Heaviness held Lisa's heart. "I'm sorry." Not only for the woman, but herself and the whole town. Daisy was such a wonderful part of her memories here in Evergreen.

"Did you know her?" the woman asked.

"Only sort of." Although in truth, Lisa felt like she'd known Daisy very well. "I was actually born here, but then we moved away when I was about seven."

"You probably would have gone to kindergarten

with my daughter Allie. She always had pigtails? Constantly chasing the animals?"

Surprisingly, she did remember a little girl like that from school. "Oddly enough, I do have a memory of that, yes. I'm Lisa Palmer."

"Palmer?" The woman's face registered recognition. "Were your parents...scientists? No, wait, they were military. Right?"

"Right on both accounts. Wow, you have a good memory." And that's how Evergreen had always seemed. Like it was a place where everyone knew you.

"I'm Carol." A man came out of the Chris Kringle Kitchen and joined them. "And this is my husband, Joe. We own the Kringle Kitchen."

"Hi," Joe said.

"Nice to meet you. I love this place." Through the window she noticed the cafe was packed, then she saw the familiar sight on the counter near the register. "And the snow globe is still here!"

Joe nodded. "It sure is. Granting wishes by the dozen. We get a lot of people from all over coming to our Christmas Eve Festival."

She hadn't even thought about the festival, although now that they'd mentioned it, she did remember the games and the whole town getting together on Christmas Eve.

"Ah! Kevin." Joe pointed to a red truck pulling in front of the cafe.

Lisa recognized the truck right away.

Carol waved. Joe said, "My vegetables." He hustled

toward the truck. Lisa found herself pleased to see Kevin again.

"Sorry I'm late. I had to deliver a few more trees." Kevin carried a crate of vegetables over to Joe. "I'll take these in."

As Kevin reached the sidewalk, Carol said, "Lisa, this is Kevin."

He stopped, smiling with a little laugh. "We met on the road. She's an astonishingly good mechanic."

Carol looked as if she'd caught them kissing rather than just having met once before.

Lisa laughed. "I gave him a little help with the truck."

"It was my dad's," Carol said. "Now it belongs to my daughter. She's in Florida visiting her boyfriend's family."

"It's a beautiful truck. A classic," Lisa said.

"Thanks. Are you hungry?"

"I'd like to get checked in over at Barbara's Country Inn." Lisa checked the address on her phone. "Is that—"

"Straight out to the end of town, take a left on Sawmill," Carol said.

"Thank you."

"Come back for dinner," Carol said.

"I will." Lisa was glad Oliver had shamed her into finally coming for a visit. Christmas in Evergreen really was the best.

Kevin walked out of the Kringle Kitchen.

"We're going to have to stop bumping into each

other like this," Lisa teased. "The townspeople will start to talk."

"That's what they do best." He opened the door of the truck and stepped on the running board. "That and harmonizing the last three bars of any Christmas carol."

Lisa smiled and got in her car. He had a great wit. *Kevin. Nice name.*

Chapter Three

C arol's directions took Lisa straight to Barbara's Country Inn, and it didn't disappoint.

The red two-story with white trim looked festive all dressed in twinkle lights and holiday decor. Even the garden archways at the entrance along the sidewalk were decorated with gold ornaments, poinsettias, and the tiny fairy lights.

Excited about staying in the charming inn, she parked in the last empty spot. *Must be a full house.* She was probably lucky to have gotten a room at the last minute. It was a good thing she'd called ahead.

A few snowflakes had started to fall as she drove over, but it was really coming down as she took her suitcase out of her car. Careful not to slip on the accumulating snow, she carried her bag, rather than rolling it, slowly stepping her way up to the house. She stomped the snow from her boots and walked inside to a glorious display of Christmas decor.

She set her suitcase down just inside the door and

closed it behind her. The warmth of the fireplace in the other room flooded the foyer, giving her a chance to relax a little from the chilly temperatures outside.

A colorful Christmas village with miniature houses, a bakery, and a church filled the entire length of the mantel in the living room, and down the hall she could see the dining room table was set with festive white and gold china. A box of Christmas ornaments on the foyer table caught her eye.

She walked over and lifted one from the box. They appeared to be fine hand-blown glass, and the craftsmanship was exquisite. For the hanger, a tiny pewter tree with a hole through the star at the top had been attached to the top of the blown glass ball. *That's a nice touch.* She held one between her fingers, admiring it.

"Oh, sorry. I meant to get those up." A brunette wearing a pink shirt and wine-colored cardigan entered the room with a smile, grabbing the box. "I got sidetracked while decorating."

"No worries. They're gorgeous. Are they handblown?" Lisa placed the ornament carefully back in the box.

"Yes." She dipped her head and looked away.

By the woman's bashful response, Lisa had to ask. "Did you make them?"

"I did."

Lisa wished she had that kind of talent. She staged stores like nobody's business, but as for handcrafting or art—she didn't have those talents. "They're exquisite."

25

"Thank you."

"Are you Barbara?" Lisa asked.

"No. I'm her sister, Megan. I'm hosting while she's away."

"Nice to meet you. I have a reservation." A woman about her own age wearing a holiday green blouse and long dark braids swept in with a laptop. "Lisa Palmer?" she asked with a bright smile.

"Yes."

"You'll be in Room 8. I'm Hannah, by the way." Her bubbly personality matched her bright smile.

"As you can see," Megan said, "it takes a team to replace my sister."

"It's my pleasure," Hannah said. "Decorating and playing Christmas is not work. I'm loving every minute of it."

"I bet. Hi, Hannah." Lisa shook her hand. "Nice to meet you." The front door opened behind her, and who stepped through the door – none other than Kevin. Again.

"Oh good," Megan said. "You brought the tree."

He wrestled the fat Fraser fir through the doorway. Lisa and Kevin's eyes met and they both laughed out loud.

"Seriously? This is getting a little weird." How many times could she possibly run into the same guy in one day? It might've worried her...if she'd been anywhere but Evergreen.

"Yeah." His eyes twinkled when he smiled. "I don't know who is following who."

Megan and Hannah looked a little baffled, but Lisa wasn't going to elaborate on her many run-ins with him.

Kevin turned to Megan. "I'll get this tree set up for you." He gave Lisa a smile and tipped an imaginary hat. "Ma'am."

Amused, Lisa laid on an elegant accent. "Sir."

Kevin hoisted the tree with ease. All three ladies watched him as he carried it into the den.

"So-oo, you've met Kevin already?" Hannah had that same look on her face that Carol had earlier.

"Yes. Three times today." As strange as it was, she wasn't sorry about it. Once Hannah gave Lisa directions to her room, Lisa climbed the stairs with her suitcase. She stopped midway, leaning over the rail to sneak another peek at Kevin.

Once she'd unpacked and was getting hungry, Lisa descended the stairs again. She paused midway, looking over the rail again to see if Kevin was still there. The tree was set up, and he was nowhere in sight. A group of guests gathered in the dining room, but Lisa had told Carol she'd come back to the diner for dinner, and really that sounded more appealing than a dinner with fancy china and silverware tonight.

Some good home cooking was exactly what she wanted.

Snow was still falling in big fat, fluffy flakes, but it had slowed significantly from earlier. She jumped in her car and revved the engine. The town was so close the car wouldn't even have time to heat up on the short drive.

She let out an audible sigh as she turned into the town square and caught the sight of Evergreen all dolled up for the holidays at night. White lights outlined every single building, and each business and office had added their own special touches. Some had toy soldiers nearly four feet tall guarding their doorways, while others had opted for candles, snowmen, or reindeer.

She got out of her car in awe of the surrounding beauty, then rocked back on her heels as she noticed the one dark spot on the block. Daisy's Country Store. It hadn't always been that way. In fact, quite the opposite. Daisy used to be the first one to deck out her store for the holidays.

As Lisa's family had been leaving Evergreen for their new home in DC all those years ago, they'd stopped here on their way out of town. It hadn't been snowing that night, but it had been bitterly cold. Mom had let her run inside to pick up something she'd called ahead for. Daisy had handed her a basket full of all of her favorite local goodies, including the candied citrus peels that Daisy had been known for making herself. Lisa hadn't wanted to leave the store that night.

Daisy had walked her out to the car, which had been packed with clothes and the few toys her parents hadn't sent along with the movers. "All packed up?" Daisy had asked.

With a shiver, Lisa relived that moment—being on the verge of tears. She'd cried most of that day. Dad had lost his patience with her pouting earlier, and Mom had been doing everything she could think of to make things better. Stopping at Daisy's had been part of that.

"Why so sad?" Daisy asked. "You're on your way to a new home and that's an awfully big adventure."

"But I don't want a new home." She loved her room at her old house, and because they were moving, Mom and Dad hadn't put up the tree in front of the window in the living room like they always had. It was like Christmas was skipping right over them. "How will Santa know how to find us?"

"Lisa, Santa knows how to find all boys and girls. No matter where you go, Christmas will find you." Daisy touched her face. "Now you have a good trip, mind your parents, and come back to visit us soon, okay?"

She'd climbed into the backseat of the car feeling like everything she knew and loved was getting ready to disappear.

"Off you go." Daisy shut the car door of Dad's big Cadillac, and waved from the sidewalk.

From the window of the back seat, she'd watched a father and son standing in the store talking near the mailbox where she'd put her letter to Santa just the week before. She'd hoped so badly that he'd receive her letter and answer her request. And she'd silently vowed she'd come back here someday.

Lisa shook off the memory, pushing her hair behind her ear like she was known to do when stressed. She had such fond memories of Daisy's store, and Daisy. She was always so kind. And wise. It was like Daisy always knew what was on her mind even though as a child she'd been too quiet to share.

She turned her back on those memories. Leaving had been hard, and this town still held a special spot in her heart.

The twinkling lights made this place feel magical. It was just like she'd remembered. The truth was, some merchants had probably changed, but she really only remembered Daisy's, the gas station, and the Kringle Kitchen. Oh, and there was a veterinarian on the block too. She only recalled that because sometimes when Dad was gassing up the car, she'd go pet the animals going in or out of the vet's office for their checkups. Dad had never let her have a pet. He said with all the moving, it wasn't fair to the animal. Lisa had always felt it was most unfair to her.

The school where she'd gone to kindergarten shouldn't be far from here, but she had no idea which direction it would be. She could picture the light blue color of the walls that led to her classroom, the smell of paste and those yummy rolls they made fresh in the cafeteria every morning. She had such treasured memories of Evergreen, and so many more surfaced now that she was here.

Lisa stepped up onto the sidewalk and went inside the Kringle Kitchen. Every table was covered in a red fabric tablecloth, with a white runner and green cloth napkins folded like Christmas trees.

At one of the first tables, an artist sat drawing a brilliant likeness of Santa Claus in a sketchbook— pretty enough to be a Christmas card.

"Hi, Lisa!" Carol met her halfway. "I didn't want you to have to eat alone." She pulled out a chair at a table near the dessert counters. Two other people were already seated at the four-topper.

"You're so sweet." Lisa sat down.

The woman seated across from her leaned forward with a smile. "I heard you went to elementary school here."

"Yes. I did."

"I'm actually the principal of the elementary school now. I'm Michelle."

"Cool." *Small world.*

"This is—" Michelle started.

"Ezra." He extended his hand. "I'm the Mayor of Evergreen."

"Nice to meet you," Lisa said. "Wow. The mayor. Well, I have to tell you your little town is the dictionary definition of charming. It is really great."

"Let's hope we can keep it that way," Ezra said with a snide glance toward Michelle.

Michelle cast a stern eye his way. "Ezra."

"Why would you say that?" Lisa asked.

"Sorry, I've been distracted. Trying to get the country store sold has been weighing on me." With a furrowed brow, Ezra took a sip of his water.

Carol came back to the table and cleared her throat. "Ezra, no business at the dinner table."

The look on Ezra's face said this wasn't the first time they had reprimanded him for doing just that.

Carol placed leather bound menus in front of each of them. "There is no stress in the Kringle Kitchen."

As soon as Carol walked away, Ezra started in. "Unless we get the country store sold, we could end up with a chain store. Or fast food. It would put smaller places like this out of business. Our tourism trade could dry up. But mainly, Evergreen wouldn't be so… Evergreen." His lips twitched.

She understood his concern. "Who owns Daisy's store now?"

Ezra looked flustered. "I do. Daisy was my godmother."

Lisa's heart pinched. "I'm sorry for your loss."

He nodded a thank-you. "Anyway, I'm looking to sell it."

She hated the possibility of Daisy's store being replaced by some big chain. She wasn't all that fond of the idea of it turning into some other kind of store, either. "You know…" She pushed up from her chair, eyeing the store through the Kringle Kitchen window. She held a finger up. "Let me just take a look at something." She walked to the other side of Ezra. That sign hanging haphazardly didn't do much for the ambiance of the place. Bare of decorations, it stood out like a rejected part among the inviting storefronts. "It could use some good staging."

Ezra jumped from his seat and leaned in close. "Staging?"

"It...yeah...staging. It's like when you're going to sell a house. You add furniture and paint a few walls just to make it look more attractive to the potential buyer."

Ezra gave a crooked smile. "Could you do that to a store?" he asked hopefully.

"Yeah. It's what I do." She had the skills to help, and why not? She had some time on her hands. "I redesign stores, sometimes add or subtract certain products. We prefer to do shops that are opening to the public, but—"

Michelle rolled her eyes. "Ezra, please let Lisa enjoy her vacation."

Lisa looked over at the store. "No, actually, I'd really like to take a look."

Ezra's mood lifted, making him seem a little more like one of Santa's playful elves than a mayor. "Daisy kept it very clean, but it's a bit of a mess inside since the snowstorm. The snow left some damage," Ezra admitted.

"I'm sure I've seen much worse." Lisa was excited to go back into the store after all these years. "Let's go take a look."

Michelle shook her head. "I'll wait here."

Lisa and Ezra walked across the street without a word, but she sensed his excitement. He took the keys from his pocket and unlocked the door. A rush of cold air stung her face as she walked inside with Ezra on her heels.

Her heart broke a little. The main components were all still there—the long wooden glass front counters, and the wood stove in the center—but it looked unloved, and that hurt.

This would take more than just a little staging. Repairs were needed too.

"During an early snowstorm, the roof practically caved in," Ezra explained.

A hole in the wall showed exposed pipes, and a huge beam had fallen, still lying catawampus across the middle of the store. The water damage had left the floors covered in thick dry dirt that flaked as she walked across it.

She sighed. "We'd need to fix that beam."

Lisa walked further inside, ducking under the beam to see the rest of the space. It was hard to not let her personal disappointment in the condition affect her vision for the possibilities. She needed to treat this place like any other retail store in need of help. There were some redeeming qualities. The old wooden phone was still on the wall, and a few antique pieces were scattered around too.

She turned to Ezra with a smile.

"We'd need to brighten the place up." She waved her hand toward the front windows. "Add some Christmas decorations. There's a lot to do if you want to sell it that quickly." Lisa walked around taking stock of what it would take.

Ezra pointed his finger in her direction. "Quick is what we're after. If I can't sell by the end of the year, the store is going to go back to the bank. They've already said they'd repossess it."

Lisa blew dust from the beam and coughed. "Well, I won't lie. It's not going to be easy, but I have seen places in worse conditions turn around on tighter schedules." She ducked under the beam. "All right." She walked back over to Ezra. They did a little do-si-do as she switched her innovative mind into high gear. "Tell you what I'll do. Point me in the direction of your town's best contractor. I'll get this place fixed up and ready to sell by Christmas."

Ezra grinned, then raised his eyebrows as he looked out the window past her. He placed his arm around Lisa's shoulder and turned her toward the window. "Kevin," he said, pointing to the man walking toward the red truck parked in front of the Kringle Kitchen, "is a contractor."

For heaven's sake. "Of course he is."

"But he's only in town for a week staying with his dad."

"Well…" She looked over her shoulder to Ezra. "I mean…I won't really need more than a week, I don't think."

"He's good," said Ezra. "Very precise."

The way Ezra said precise, Lisa wasn't entirely sure if it was a compliment or not. But she took that as reason enough to talk to Kevin about what it would take to get the store staged in the short time they had.

It wouldn't be an easy job, but she couldn't let Daisy's just end like this. *I can do this.* She raced out of the store to catch Kevin before he left.

Chapter Four

Kevin had just opened the door of the red truck to put things in the passenger seat when he caught sight of the blonde woman from that morning. She wore jeans and a leather jacket that was cute, but not very practical in such cold weather. This time she was coming out of Daisy's Country Store.

He was surprised to see anyone coming from the building since it was out of business, and he was even more surprised that it was her of all people. Again. It was a small town, but he'd never run into someone this many times in one day. He wondered what her connections were to Evergreen, and Daisy's for that matter.

"Kevin!" She jogged across the town square toward him. "Hi."

He closed the door, still holding a yellow rag. "Hey."

"So, let's just say I was going to start a project where I needed someone handy with tools."

Was she talking about fixing up that place? Kevin looked over at Daisy's Country Store. It held a lot of special memories for him, too, but that place needed more than just a few tools to fix it. He wiped his hands on the rag. "You're going to buy Daisy's store?" *That would explain why she was here.*

"What?" She looked confused. "Oh, no. I'm going to fix it up for Christmas and get it ready for a buyer."

"No." He shook his head. "Just throwing a few decorations up won't help." He tossed the rag back into the truck. "That place needs a lot of work." Was she crazy?

Lisa gave him a pleading look. "Which is why I need someone to help me do that."

Kevin leaned against the truck and folded his arms. "And you think I'm your man?" He should be so lucky. Then again, getting involved with a visitor wasn't in the cards for him. He still hadn't decided whether to take that job with the logging company or not, and he just didn't have the time to spend on a relationship.

She gave him a playful wiggle of her shoulders. "I have no idea if you're my man or not." She lifted her brow. "But I'm willing to bet you care about this place as much as any of these other people."

"I do." Kevin looked at the store. Everyone had been so sad when it closed. Even more so when Daisy had passed away. "And what makes *you* care about it?"

She stood there for a long quiet moment.

He'd expected to hear something quick and quippy from her. Instead, she looked around then raised her hands and shrugged. "Because I have some pretty special memories here too." The words were softer. Personal.

Kevin smiled and nodded. The sincere answer had surprised him. He had many special memories of Daisy and the store too. Penny candy, coloring contests, and dropping off letters to Santa. Old memories. Even as far back as the year Mom passed away.

He reminded himself he had plenty on his plate, and it was the holidays. Besides, fixing up the store was an incredibly huge undertaking, and she was on a tight schedule.

She clasped her hands together, nearly begging. "Look. Take a week and help me do this. We'll be done before Christmas."

"Sorry, I can't." He wished he could help her. She was hard to turn down, but this was nuts. He stepped around her toward the old country store. It had once been a pretty cool place, and spending time with her to fix it up was appealing, but there wasn't enough time no matter how he looked at it. "It's...that's not enough time to get it done right," he said with his back to her.

"What are you talking about? Of course we have enough time. I have tons of experience, and I'm sure that you...have...some experience too. Right?"

She was grasping at straws, but she wasn't wrong.

Even with his back to her, he heard the hope in her words.

"Yes." He turned around to face her, and she flashed

that pretty smile of hers. He did have a lot of experience with this kind of stuff. The work, that is. Not that smile that was making him a bit off-kilter right now. He rubbed his neck. "Yes. I started out doing freelance construction gigs. Over time, people found out that I'm pretty good at leading a team, have a good eye for detail, that kind of thing." His dad would've preferred to have him stick around and run the family farm, but that just hadn't satisfied him. Maybe because he'd grown up around it. Plus, after Mom died, he and Dad hadn't been able to see eye-to-eye on anything. It had been easier to just find his own way, doing something he was good at and enjoyed. "After a while word got around, and now, I get calls from all over. People bring me in as a sort of foreman-for-hire. I just finished a library in Denver."

Lisa practically jumped like a cheerleader. "See, you're perfect for this."

"But look," he said stepping closer. "Even if you had a whole fleet of magical helpers to help—"

Lisa cut in. "Which I don't, but I'm willing to bet you know some people who—"

"Who I would have a hard time getting to work over the holiday."

"Not if you told them that it's a Christmas gift for the entire town." Her voice was sing-songy and there was that smile again.

"Wow." He lowered his head and laughed. "You are *really* persistent."

"Yes I am." She clapped her hands together, looking more serious. "I am."

"Okay, so what's in it for you, if you don't mind me asking?"

"I don't know." She shook her head. "It just feels like something I should do." Appearing almost desperate, she said, "Plus, I was told by Ezra that you're the best contractor in this town."

Not exactly a compliment. "I'm the *only* contractor in this town right now."

"Yeah." She pressed her lips together. "There is that." She let out a sigh, then grounded her stance. "I can promise you that we will be fast."

That was not what he wanted to hear. "No." He raised his hand. "If we're going to do this, it can't be rushed or thrown together." Why did he feel like he was getting ready to give in? Bad idea. It was too big of a job to get done before the holiday. There was that twinkle in her eye again.

Her gaze held his for a beat. Then, she waved her hands. "No. No-no. Not rushed or thrown together. We will work fast, but smart." Their eyes still locked, she thrust her hand in his direction. "Deal?"

Kevin looked down at her hand, then at the store. When he looked back at Lisa, she was grinning ear to ear. "Deal."

They shook hands, but he had a suspicion he might be in for more than he'd bargained for.

Chapter Five

First thing the next morning, Lisa met Kevin at Daisy's Country Store to talk through the project, do a quick inventory of the immediate repairs needed, and get things rolling.

"We don't have a lot of time," Lisa said. "I figure we'll start with the safety issues and non-negotiables, then I'll walk you through the space and share my vision and we can prioritize from there."

"Sounds good." Kevin dipped his head toward the beam in the middle of the room. "That's a priority."

"For sure." She cringed slightly. "Any idea how much that's going to cost?"

"I've got a guy who is really good with this kind of stuff. I texted him this morning. I'm hoping he can meet us out here sometime this afternoon and give us a price." He cocked his head. "Hopefully, he'll have some time to work on it."

She held her hand up and crossed her fingers. "It'll work out. I know it."

A walkthrough of the store identified a leaky faucet and a few electrical issues, but for the most part it was a list of things that needed to be nailed down or tightened up. "It's not so bad," Kevin said. "Considering how long it's been empty."

"That's great news. So if we can work smart and fast, clearing an area at a time, I can start staging as we complete the sections."

"That sounds good."

She turned her back on him and spread her arms out to the side. "Now, what I see is brightening the place up. White paint. Lots of it. We'll paint out the long counter on the left side here. The whole thing. On the right side, we'll just paint the bottom of the counter white, leaving the wooden tops to kind of pop against the white. The four wooden steps up to the second level. All white."

"Agree."

"The floors." Her mouth twisted in disgust. "I'm not even sure what to do with them. They are such a mess."

"Water-damaged, too."

"Yeah. I'd thought we'd sand them and polyurethane them, but I think they are way past a quick sanding. They are almost black in some spots." She winced at the thought of how long it would take to really fix them. She looked at him hoping for the best.

"What's Plan B?"

She was afraid of that. She'd been hoping he might have an easy solution for the floors, but in her gut she'd known there wasn't one. "Sand them enough to get them smooth, then paint white and black checkerboard." She turned and pressed her finger to her lips. "Or I guess we could put down black-and-white tiles."

"No tiles. That would be a nightmare to remove for the new owner. No short cuts either. Painting would be the better option, but we need to give it enough time to cure and it'll need a couple coats of clear to withstand the foot traffic."

"You're right." She appreciated the balance he brought to the plans. "We don't have much time."

"I have some heaters and fans that'll help it dry a little faster. I think it would really look good and still give that old-time warmth you're going for. We'd have to paint in the evenings, and let it dry overnight."

"That would work." What a relief. "Oh, and where the glass cases are damaged on the second level, let's use wainscoting to cover that up. It's a quick fix, but a good one. It'll look nicer and offer storage."

"Storage is always a selling point," Kevin agreed. "You can never have too much storage."

"Which brings me to the storage room. Let's clear out as much as we can and give that room a quick coat of white. We'll reload in boxes that are labeled so it looks roomy and organized."

He followed her through the store as she relayed her vision, but he didn't say much. Finally, they'd walked every inch of the store and come to an agreement on what needed to happen.

With the short list of what they needed to purchase immediately in her hand, and the long list tucked in her purse to review later, they walked out of the store. While they'd been planning inside, out here the local merchants had transformed the sidewalks and open space into something wonderful with kiosks and tented booths with all kinds of goodies and gifts. Festive instrumental music played from the speakers in the nearby gazebo.

Oliver had called Evergreen an almost-real-life-Santa's Village. It really wasn't so far-fetched an assessment this morning. *All we need is Santa.*

On the corner down from the Kringle Kitchen, Joe stood next to a colorful chalkboard sign with "Hot Cocoa" written on it. Set up like a hot chocolate bar, there were all kinds of goodies to snazz up the cocoa—everything from candy canes and marshmallows, to whipped cream and sprinkles. Joe poured piping hot cups from a red carafe to happy customers under his red and white striped awning.

Joe greeted Lisa and Kevin as they walked up. "Good morning! What can I get for you?"

Lisa eyed the display. "I would love a peppermint hot cocoa, please."

Joe poured. "Right in on the Christmas spirit, good for you. And you, Kevin? What can I get for you?"

"Coffee. Just black," he said.

Lisa sighed inwardly. Joe's face fell, then he looked at Kevin like he'd committed a crime.

"Please?" Kevin said with a shrug. "What?"

"'Tis the season, Kevin," Joe said. It had come out more of a scold than a salutation.

"Yeah," Lisa chided. "Live a little."

"Okay. Fine." Kevin looked at the list of the things on the chalkboard menu. "Coffee with whipped cream, then."

Joe finally smiled. "Caramel?"

"No." Kevin glanced over at Lisa, who cocked her head and gave him an exaggerated nod. "Wait. Yes. Please."

Lisa laughed. At least he'd taken the hint, although it had been far from subtle.

While Joe made their order, Lisa started rattling off the things on her list. "I want to get some decorations, and I would love to stop by a Christmas tree lot. Do you guys have one of those?"

"We have five."

"You have five?"

"Yeah." Kevin appeared to be very proud of that little fact. "It's going to be a tough choice, but I'm probably going to push for the one my dad runs."

Lisa enjoyed the playful small talk. "Ah. Yes. Your dad's place is probably a pretty safe bet."

"He'll appreciate that."

"Good. And you know what, I was thinking we could use a tree on the outside, and then a smaller one on the inside."

Kevin's eyes narrowed. "You don't think two trees is a bit much?"

"Ambition is the key to success."

He shook his head, and the look on his face said it all. He thought she was half nuts. He'd get used to her positive vibe eventually. Hopefully, sooner rather than later. Mr. Play-It-Safe would have to agree once she proved she was right.

Lisa paid Joe for the order.

"All right. Here you go." He handed Lisa a cup of cocoa with marshmallows and a peppermint candy cane hanging over the side. "Merry Christmas."

"Thank you. Merry Christmas to you," she said as Joe handed the cup of coffee to Kevin.

"Thanks, Joe." He took a quick sip as he and Lisa turned and headed back down the street.

"Now. First things first," Lisa said. "We need a good window display. And supplies." She swirled the peppermint stick in her cocoa then stuck it in her mouth.

"I've got a guy," Kevin said.

"I knew you were the right man for the job." Lisa followed Kevin to his truck, and they drove over to the local hardware store.

When they got out of the truck, Lisa pulled her green coat tighter around her as the wind picked up. Stacks of firewood lined the left side of the front entrance. On the right, forty-pound bags of ice melt were stacked chest-high next to a bin of snow shovels with bright red blades. She pulled the short list out of her pocket as they walked inside.

Evergreen Village Hardware was decorated for Christmas and cramped for space. Like most old buildings, the aisles were tight, making for a lot of excuse-me's and side-passing one another.

Lisa led the way in, then turned around, walking backward to face Kevin. "Okay, so I'd like to get some pine garland, lots of white paint, and the wainscoting and…" She stopped in front of a set of tomato cages that had been decorated like Christmas trees. Only for ornaments, someone had decorated paintbrushes to look like Santas, elves, snowmen, and even a red-handled brush with a big black belt and gold buckle. "That is so cute!"

"Interesting." Kevin didn't sound nearly as impressed as she was.

They rounded the corner and came across two men talking. One of them, who looked astonishingly like Santa Claus on vacation, glanced their way.

"Oh. Ho ho. Hello. Nice to see you, Kevin," he said.

"You too. Lisa, this is Phil, he runs the hardware store, and this is Nick, who plays Santa at the festival every year."

"I can see why." Lisa had never seen a better Santa in her life. Oliver's assessment of Evergreen had proved to be completely accurate. "Nice to meet you, Nick."

Nick had a twinkle in his eye. "What brings you two out on such a chilly morning?"

"Little project we're working on together," Kevin said.

"Sounds like my cue to leave you in Phil's quite capable hands," Nick said with a twinkle in his eye. He waved and left with a lift in his step.

The owner of Evergreen Village Hardware clapped his hand into Kevin's. "Good to see you. How are you doing?"

"Great. Busy as usual. We're working on the project to repair and stage Daisy's to help Ezra sell it."

"Hi, Phil." Lisa shook his hand. "So nice to meet you."

"What can I help you with?"

Kevin jumped in. "A ten-gallon bucket of white interior paint. Wainscoting. How much do you have in stock?"

Phil led them to the aisle with lumber, paneling and wainscoting. "I've got six sheets in stock, but I can have more in a couple of days if you need it."

"We'll take those six with us. We'll need more. And the lady needs some fresh garland."

"That's outside in the garden area. Plenty of it. Pine. Fir. Cedar. Lots to pick from."

Lisa clapped her hands, delighted that the store was so well stocked. It didn't look all that big from the road, but inside they hadn't wasted an inch of space. "Great." She went outside and picked out garland, mixing it up with some long-needled pine roping and tighter cedar garland. Together they'd look nice and full. "We're going to need a cart back here."

"I'm on it." Kevin went to get a cart and she started piling things together.

She couldn't pass up a crate of pinecones for five bucks, then grabbed a couple cans of decorative snow flocking to go with them. You could never go wrong with snow flocking.

Kevin rounded the corner with the cart, putting his foot on the frame and skating it the last six feet. "You work fast."

"I told you. Fast, but smart."

"Right." He started loading up her finds.

"See? Small stores are the best. Look at this." She lifted a box and carried it to the cart. "Faux magnolia flowers. These will be a gorgeous addition. So much better than the expected poinsettias this time of year." She plopped the box on top. "I'm going to grab a roll of fishing line if they have any. It is a must-have on these kinds of decorating jobs."

Phil walked over. "Aisle four," he said. "On the end cap."

She dashed off and snatched a box. Waving it in the air, she caught back up with Kevin and Phil.

"Looks like you're finding everything okay," Phil said. "We've got the other stuff loaded in the truck already. Anything else I can do for you?"

"One more thing." She lifted her finger and gave a flirty nod toward Kevin. "Phil, does the hardware store have a miscellaneous box?"

Phil gave her a wink. "Wouldn't be a hardware store without one." He called over to one of his helpers to load lumber for one of the other customers, then led her toward the back. Behind the counter in front of a wall full of tape measures, wrenches, and other hand tools, Phil lifted a series of wooden boxes up onto the counter. "Have at it."

"Thank you. This is great." Delighted, she started digging through one of the boxes.

Phil seemed to be getting a kick out of her delight, and Kevin hadn't wasted a second before he dove in himself.

"Don't you love how hardware stores have these boxes full of stuff they just don't know what to do with?" Lisa said as she sifted through her box.

"Yeah, I try to raid these boxes wherever I go."

She popped up and looked him square in the eye. "You do too?"

"Yes."

"I love it. You never know what you're going to find." It amazed her how two people who were so obviously so different could have so much in common. She moved to a box of old picture frames, lifting one up and setting it aside.

Kevin pulled a small box toward him then looked up at Phil. "What are all these keys?"

"Well, we don't know what any of them actually go to," Phil said. "But you know every time you throw out a key, you find a lock that it might fit."

Kevin lifted a large hand-sized key from the box. The dark bronze looked heavy and had an ornate "S" at the top. "What about this one?"

Kevin held it up, then looked to Lisa. Her eyes widened.

"Hmm. Had to have been here long before my day," Phil said. "Anything you find here in these boxes you can have for a nickel apiece."

They smiled at each other. *Jackpot!* This was exactly why she loved looking through these old junk boxes. "Are you sure?"

"Christmas discount." Phil winked at Lisa.

This is my day. She reached across to shake Phil's hand. "Deal."

A lot less picky at this point, Lisa filled her hands with the old treasures, even piling a few things into Kevin's arms. The picture frames would come in handy filling up the empty shelves in Daisy's.

She rummaged through the box full of keys. "Can you imagine all the different kinds of things these went to?" If there were a story written for every one of these keys, she could read for years.

Satisfied that the one Kevin had found was the most unique, she gathered her bounty. "Ready to go?"

"Yeah. We did good."

"Darn right we did." She couldn't have planned a shopping trip to be as fun as this. As she followed him through the store, she noticed how the muscles in his arms flexed as he carried their treasures. Her eyes on him, and not on where she was going, her hip caught the edge of a display, sending a stack of three-inch round peat pots bouncing to the ground.

She quickly gathered them, then quick-stepped

to catch up. They made their way to the front of the store where Phil rang them up. As she got to the passenger side of the truck, she caught a whiff of the fresh garland.

It's beginning to feel like Christmas.

Chapter Six

Back at Daisy's Country Store, Lisa and Kevin unloaded the items they'd just bought, then carried the wainscoting inside, stacking it in the back of the store.

Lisa looked at the big box of cleaning supplies that Ezra had dropped off for them. "I know that first and foremost I should get down to cleaning this place, and you've got a long list of fixes to get going on, but how would you feel about helping me put up the garland outside? I mean, this place is the only dark spot on the block at night. It needs a Christmas boost. It'll look more cheerful and that will make us happy as we work, right?"

A dimple formed as his lips tugged into a smile. "How can a guy say no to helping make things cheerful and happy?"

"Exactly." She grabbed the new staple gun they'd just bought and loaded it with staples. "If you can help me with the stuff across the front of the building, I promise I'll take care of the rest on my own."

"Don't go making promises you can't keep," he warned.

"Good point." He was teasing her, but she couldn't help but think there were a few other promises she wouldn't mind making to someone like him.

She shook off the unexpected thought. She needed to keep her focus on the project at hand. No matter how great he seemed, she was only in town for a short time and long-distance would never work. She liked her carefree schedule and lifestyle.

"I'd like to also string those blue lights across the front," she said.

"See." He wagged a finger at her. "The list is already growing. I'll get the ladder."

"And the lights. They are in the box next to the staircase."

"I'll get them."

She picked up the staple gun, then gathered up some of the garland and moved it back outside. Unrolling one of the bunches, she spread the long-needled pine roping out across the front of the store to measure how much she'd need. Two tied together would give her just enough length to give it a little swag. She went to work connecting the two pieces end to end, then added a layer of the cedar garland on top of it, twisting them together as she went, and securing it every couple of feet with some fishing line. The garland left her hands sticky. She rubbed her hands together, trying to work the sap from them. "So much better."

"Are you talking to yourself?" He set the box of lights outside the door.

"Don't you?" Lisa picked up a can of the snow flocking and gave it a good shake before giving the garland a light mist. "If we add a few magnolias and pine cones to this, it's going to look like a million bucks."

"I'll have to take your word for that," Kevin said.

She rummaged through a box nearby, then held up a magnolia in one hand and a pine cone in the other. "Well, we happen to have both. So you'll see for yourself in just a minute."

He went back inside to get the ladder and when he came out, she was ready to hang the garland across the front. Kevin set up the ladder at the far end of the porch.

She lifted the one end of her modified garland and handed him the staple gun. He secured the end and placed another staple about two feet in.

Lisa ran down to the middle section of the garland. "Staple this in the middle next. Then we can work back from there."

"Why would we do that? I can just pull it tight as I go."

A crease formed on her forehead. "No. You can't do that. It has to hang a little. You know, have kind of a swoop to it."

"No. I guess I didn't know." He climbed down the ladder, amused.

"Yeah, yeah." She waved him over, and he picked up the ladder and moved to the center of the porch right below the center of the Daisy's Country Store sign.

Before he stepped a foot on the ladder, she gave him a hand gesture to move the ladder over another six inches or so. He didn't look convinced, but he did it.

She lifted the center of the garland and handed it to him, then stood at the bottom of the ladder, supervising the process.

"That looks so good."

"I think this side is a little too low," he said.

"I will always err on the side of quaint over symmetrical," Lisa explained.

He shook his head. As he hung the decorative garland across the front, the store began to shape up.

She stepped back and looked up. Once the lights were up, the whole town would start getting excited about the staging, and hopefully the ultimate sale of the store would happen to someone with something in mind that fit perfectly here in Evergreen.

"We need to give the garland a little floof so the two types mingle more naturally together." She waved her hands in a floofing motion.

He looked at her like she was crazy. "Floof?"

"Is there another ladder? If we're both up there you'll see what I mean and we can work on it faster."

"I saw a shorter ladder by the furnace." He climbed down. "I'll go get it."

As soon as he made it through the front door she climbed to the top of the ladder and started arranging.

Kevin walked out of the store carrying the ladder. "I noticed Santa's mailbox. I think we might want to put that somewhere so it doesn't get messed up. That mailbox was a very special tradition in this store."

"I know. You're right. I'd hate it if anything happened to it." Even though her letter to Santa hadn't been answered exactly, she still held that old tradition close to her heart. "Maybe I can get Carol and Joe to let us house it over at the Kringle Kitchen until we get Daisy's in good shape."

"Good plan." Kevin took a step back into the street, then frowned. "You're not going to be happy about this, but your garland is not centered." He gave it a so-so hand gesture. "The center is a little—"

"It's a little off. I know," she said. "But that just adds a little more interest. It'll hold the eye. Trust me. I know what I'm doing."

He put the ladder next to hers and stepped up on it. "But it's…" Her arm brushed his hair, and the movement made him look up. Her blue eyes sparkled and her hair fell softly across her cheek as their eyes met.

Realizing just how close he was to her, a tingle swirled through her. She smiled, not knowing exactly what to do.

"So if we just—" He fidgeted, then stepped down

off the ladder. "Yeah, you know what you're doing. Where should I staple?"

She came down off of the taller ladder and handed him the staple gun. "Just about every five feet. Then let it hang loose a little."

He lifted the garland and let it swag a little. "Here?"

"Very nice." And very nice was how it felt being that close to him. She cleared her throat. "So I should move the mailbox."

"At least until the guys get the beam fixed and we get things painted," he said without making eye contact with her again. "Let's get those lights strung. I don't have to do any floofing or swooping with those, do I?"

"Perfectly straight will be perfectly fine." Ezra was right about Kevin. He liked things precise. She could let him have a string of straight lights. *Don't let it be said I never compromise.*

It must be nice to meet someone and hit it off instantly. Michelle had noticed the chemistry between Lisa and Kevin the first time she met them. She swirled a red, green and white candy cane in her hot chocolate as she and Carol watched Lisa and Kevin decorate the front of Daisy's from the window by the register in the Kringle Kitchen.

Kevin stood on a ladder twisting bulbs into a strand of blue Christmas lights he and Lisa had just hung across the front of the store. He dropped one of

59

the blue light bulbs, barely missing Lisa's head. They both laughed as they watched him stoop down from the ladder, clearly apologizing. Lisa bent down and picked up the bulb and handed it to him, giving him a playful swat on the arm as he took it from her.

"They're sweet together," Carol mused as she watched.

Joe popped up out of nowhere between Carol and Michelle. "Don't go stirring the pot, Carol," he said, shaking his head.

"I do not stir the pot, Joe." She leaned back and placed her left hand on his cheek, then kissed the other.

Michelle drew back. "Carol Shaw, you tried to set me up with no less than three people last year alone." She placed a hand on Carol's shoulder and walked back to her table.

"Yes." She wiped her hands on a towel and set it on the counter. "But I stopped," she insisted. "As soon as you told me you weren't interested."

"Yeah, right." Carol would never stop matchmaking, it was just part of who she was.

The door to the cafe opened and Hannah bounded in with a big smile, followed closely by a man and young boy. "Hey guys."

"Hey, Welcome back." Carol walked over to greet them.

"Thanks. You remember my older brother, Thomas." She hugged the young boy at her side. "And my nephew, David."

Joe stood next to the Christmas tree holding a red carafe. "Yes, of course. Thomas, it's good to have you back."

"It's good to be back," Thomas said.

Michelle couldn't take her eyes off the tall, bald, and charming Thomas as he stood there in a nice pullover and winter coat next to his son. Joe was tall, but Thomas was an easy few inches taller than him.

"We've missed the Kringle Kitchen and your incredible apple dumplings," he said to Carol.

"Why, thank you." Then with that mischievous smile on her face, Carol grabbed Thomas by the arm, practically dragging him across the cafe. "Have you met Michelle?"

Hannah looked confused, and Michelle could've died when Carol finally stopped right beside her chair.

Michelle stood, trying to roll with the awkward moment. *Carol's at it again!*

"The famous Michelle?" Thomas nodded to his sister. "Hannah talks about you all the time, and somehow we haven't met."

"Yeah, we're always missing each other when you're in town, I guess." Michelle licked her lips. She hoped she didn't look as flustered as she felt right this moment, especially with Carol gawking over the two of them. "Nice to meet you."

"Yes." Thomas was quiet for a second too long, giving Carol another opening.

"Well, come on. Take your coat off." Carol tugged on his coat sleeve, then pulled out the chair next to Michelle. "Have a seat right over here next to Michelle." She scurried behind Michelle. "And let's bring this table over and get you two all cozy too," she said to Hannah and David.

Hannah helped move the tables together.

Carol rushed off and came back with a pot of coffee in a flash, warming up Michelle's coffee first. She eyed Michelle. "So, Thomas. Correct me if I'm wrong, but you and David spend Christmas here every...*other* year. Right?"

"Right. My ex-wife and I, we trade off Christmases."

Carol eyed Michelle. "I see."

Carol's smile was wide as she did a slow turn away, making sure Michelle saw the "go-get-him" look in her eye.

No. You're not a pot stirrer, Carol. Right.

Michelle laughed nervously, but thankfully Thomas was laughing too.

The bells on the Kringle Kitchen door jingled, and in walked Lisa carrying the bright red Santa's mailbox from Daisy's.

Hannah called from the table, "Hey Lisa, why don't you come on over and join us?"

Lisa set the mailbox on the counter and made her way to their table.

"This is my brother, Thomas, and my nephew, David," Hannah said. The lanky boy nodded a hello.

"Hi, it's nice to meet you." Lisa unbuttoned her coat.

"So, how's the store update coming?" Michelle asked, relieved the focus was off her for now.

"Well..." She took off her coat and sat down holding the fancy key in her hand. "It's a work in progress. We're getting there."

David leaned forward. "What's that?"

His wide-eyed interest seemed to tickle Lisa.

"This?" Lisa turned the fancy bronze key over in her hand. "This is a key that Kevin and I found at the hardware store. I still haven't found a place to put it yet though."

"What does it go to?" he asked.

"That is a very, very good question. I don't know. It could go to anything in this town really." She looked around the table. "It's kind of like a little puzzle."

"I love puzzles. How are you going to figure it out?" David's eyes danced with excitement as he wiggled in his seat. "It sounds like you'd have to try every keyhole in town."

"Right?" Lisa feigned being overwhelmed. "I mean that sounds like a lot of work, huh? Just imagine all the locks this key could open." She played it up. "I just wish I had somebody that would maybe..."

David leaned in closer to her, flashing his best smile.

"Wait a minute. Would you want to try it?" She held the key out in her hand.

David practically leapt from his chair. "Yes!"

"Yeah?"

"Yes!" he repeated, twice as excited.

"Okay."

He looked to his Dad. "I mean, can I?"

"Yeah. Sure. Go for it."

"All right. There you go." Lisa handed him the key. "Good luck."

His eyes widened as he turned the fancy old skeleton key over in his hands, seeming to imagine the possibilities. "Whoa. Thank you!"

"You're welcome," Lisa said sweetly.

"Where should we start, Aunt Hannah?"

"Me?" Hannah looked like she hadn't realized she was getting hoodwinked into puzzle-solving too. "Maybe we start with Town Hall. Maybe there are some records of old buildings we can check."

Carol came to the table carrying a white platter. "Hot apple dumplings. No calories," she teased as she set them down in the center of the table.

The rich aroma from the apples and pastry with the sugary drizzle on top wafted across the table. No one said no to Carol's hot apple dumplings. They were craved for miles around, and people would drive an hour out of their way to stop back by the Kringle Kitchen on their trips just for the sweet treat.

David licked his lips. "I remember these from last time we were here. They're the best." He looked at the key in his hand. "Can we eat first?" He looked at Hannah.

"Well, we're going to need our strength to hunt down the lock. We definitely need to eat some apple dumplings before we go."

David pumped his fist. "Yes!"

Michelle started cutting and serving the hot apple dumplings around the table. The warm spices mingled in the air. They smelled so good that the people at the table behind them were already ordering apple dumplings for their table too.

"Oh, Carol," Lisa said. "I need to ask you something." She got up and walked over to the counter at the front of the store. "So. Kevin and I thought it might be a good idea to keep Santa's mailbox in a safe place while we are working across the street. We were hoping that maybe you would let us keep it over here."

"We'll find room, of course." Carol took the mailbox from Lisa, but as she lifted the mailbox from the stand a letter fell to the ground.

"Oh?" Carol stooped down to pick it up. "What's this?"

"Looks like a..." Lisa lifted her foot, trying not to step on it. "It looks like a letter. To Santa. Maybe it got stuck under there." The paper was yellowed with age. "It's old, though."

"Are you going to read it?" Carol coaxed Lisa.

"Well, no. I mean, that's someone's Christmas wish."

"Yeah," said Carol.

Michelle spoke up. "I would definitely open it."

"Looks like it's already open," David said.

"It's open, but it's a matter of whether we read it or we don't." Lisa bit down on her lower lip. "I don't know. It seems so personal. Do you really think we should?"

Carol raised her hand in the air. "All in favor."

Everyone raised their hands without hesitation.

Lisa sputtered, and laughed.

"Come on," Carol led her back to her chair.

"Okay." She sat down. "All right." She took the letter out of the envelope and unfolded it. "It's typed. And it's dated."

Carol moved in closer, leaning over Lisa's shoulder. "That's twenty-five years old. It's been in that store that long."

"Wow. Okay." Lisa held the letter between her hands. "It says, Dear Santa. T is year, I ust want …" She stopped. "Wait a minute. It looks like some of the letters didn't work very well on that typewriter. The H and the J. So, let me try this again."

She started back at the top of the letter, reading slowly.

"Dear Santa. This year, I just want Christmas like it used to be. I'm sure you know it's been a tough year. It would be nice to have Christmas like it used to be. With the candles and the carols and the bells. This Christmas, just this once, I want it to go back to the way it was. Best wishes, K M."

The gang all sat quiet for a moment, their hearts a little touched.

"Who's KM?" David asked. Thomas and Hannah both shrugged.

The answer came to Michelle, tugging at her heartstrings. "Kevin Miller," she said quietly.

Lisa looked out the window at Kevin, who was still working on the lights across the street.

"And the candles and the carols and the bells?" Lisa asked, turning back to Michelle. "What is that talking about?"

As close as Lisa and Kevin appeared, Michelle imagined Lisa probably had quite a few questions running through her head right now. "Those are all things we used to do in the town. Before Daisy was the main Christmas event planner, Ruth Miller was."

Lisa held the letter tight. "And Ruth Miller is…"

"Was…Kevin's mom." Michelle remembered Ruth well.

"And his letter never made it to Santa," David said.

"No. It didn't." Carol placed a gentle hand on David's shoulder.

"I'm going to head back over to Daisy's and help Kevin," Lisa said. "Thanks for taking care of Santa's mailbox, Carol."

"You're welcome."

Lisa jogged across the street, already giving directions to Kevin before she reached the other side of it.

Michelle and Carol exchanged a glance. There was certainly some kind of spark between Lisa and Kevin.

Joe walked over to the table again. "I see you're eyeing our snow globe, David."

"It's all he's talked about the whole ride here."

Thomas let out a hearty laugh. "Making a wish on the snow globe and doing puzzles with his Aunt Hannah."

David looked embarrassed. "Yeah, and now Hannah and I have a real puzzle to solve." He held up the key. "But I do want to wish on that magic snow globe."

"Then let's get you started on the wishing." Joe led David over to the front counter. "Now the key to it is that you have to wish for what your heart really wants. The true wish of your heart."

David nodded his head quickly. "I know what I'm going to wish for."

"Oh, you're ready then." Under the direction of Joe, David picked up the snow globe, turned it over and shook it vigorously.

Michelle saw Thomas flinch. He was probably afraid his son was going to drop the famed snow globe. She had the same worry herself when she wished on it last year about this time.

A few moments later, David walked back over to the table with a smile a mile wide.

"What'd you wish for?" his dad asked.

Michelle watched as father and son spoke.

"If you tell it, it won't come true," David said.

"Oh?" Thomas let it go. "Fair enough."

He seemed like a good dad, Michelle thought. It must be hard to only have your son every other Christmas. At least they were guaranteed to have a memorable one here in Evergreen.

Chapter Seven

The next morning a heavy frost still covered the ground. Kevin had spent a lot of Christmases in Evergreen, but this one seemed the coldest and snowiest of all. He pulled up in front of the inn to pick up Lisa. Before he could get out of the truck, she was already heading his way. She jumped into the passenger seat with a cheery, "Good morning."

"Good morning. Thanks for coming with me." He'd texted her this morning, thinking she might enjoy the decorating, plus they could iron out some of the plans for Daisy's. He backed out of the driveway and headed over to Main Street. "I try to help out the church ladies when I can. I promised I'd hang wreaths for them today."

"Sure thing. I'm a great helper." She blew in her hands and rubbed them together. "It's brisk out there today. Where are we headed?"

"You'll see. It's not far." Kevin was pretty sure she'd recognize the way back to town. He pulled the truck along the side of the road, across the street from the church. "We're here."

"That didn't take long."

He got out of the truck, and so did she. He waited for her to come around to the street side of the truck, then took her hand and jogged across the street. The tiny Evergreen Church sat nestled between giant old cedar trees, just behind the town square across from the gazebo.

"It's so pretty."

He nodded. "Did I mention we might be hanging some of these wreaths outside?" Condensation formed a puff of smoke as he spoke.

"Uh, no, but I don't mind." As they got closer to the church, Lisa stopped. "With the snow and wreaths on the door, the church looks like it was straight out of a fairy tale. Quaint. Like a picture."

"It's a great old church. In the spring lots of couples show up in Evergreen just to wed in the church or over in the gazebo. There's a storybook look and feel to the place that draws people in from all over, since destination weddings have become such a big thing."

"I can see how that might be the case," Lisa said. "I could imagine getting married in a cute little church like this. Not too big. Special."

"It is." It surprised him a little that a beautiful and caring woman like Lisa had never been married. Of course, maybe that was her choice, but she was definitely a catch.

"I'll show you around," he said. They walked

inside through the tall fairy-tale doors at the front of the church.

He led her through a door to the right that took them downstairs into the basement, turning to spot her down the last step. "I'm usually out managing a job right up until Christmas, so I don't always get this much time in town."

The space was filled with boxes labeled "Christmas Festival Arts and Crafts" and plastic tubs stacked two and three high all around the room. There were several people down here moving things around and stacking things, presumably to make room for more.

"Hey, you guys," Kevin said to Hannah and David.

"Hi," they said.

Lisa looked under the lid of one of the tubs. "What is all this stuff?"

Hannah answered from across the way. "Every year at the Christmas Festival, we have our local arts and crafts fair. We store everything here before we set up the booths. Like these…" She grabbed a bright red knit hat with a pom-pom on top out of one of the boxes and tugged it onto her head. "Are my hats." She posed.

"I love them." Lisa admired a handcrafted snow owl she'd taken out of a box. It seemed to be made out of some kind of wood or buri needles. "That's nice. There's a lot of good stuff in here." Lisa walked over to join Hannah and David, who was still holding that old key in his hand.

"This is one of the oldest buildings in Evergreen."

David held up the key. "I've tried the key on all the locks. So far. Nothing." He was clearly disappointed, and Hannah gave him a hug. He dragged his feet as he walked over to the bell mechanism where Kevin stood.

Then David looked up. "Wow."

Lisa joined them, and Kevin motioned for her to look up, too. From there, she could see straight up the tower to the bells that hung below the steeple.

"Wow. Beautiful." She stood there staring at the bells for a long moment.

"Daisy always wanted to get the bells working again." Kevin tugged on one of the heavy ropes, but it barely budged. "My dad tried for a while. But nobody knows exactly what's wrong with the mechanism." He eyed the cogs and gears. "It just stopped working one day."

Lisa walked over to examine the gears and mechanisms that seem to be tied to the church bells.

"Come on, Aunt Hannah," David said. "Let's go see if the people at the bank might know where this key goes."

"All right. Let's go." She let him take her by the hand and drag her toward the stairs.

Kevin and Lisa waved as they left. "See you guys," they said together.

Kevin looked up at the steeple with a sense of melancholy. These bells had meant so much to his mom. To everybody. They'd been part of the tradition in this town. He glanced over at Lisa, who was watching him. "You said you were born here, so do you remember the bells ringing?"

"That was so long ago. It's all hazy. We moved around to so many towns, they started to blend together," she said. "However, I do remember Evergreen the most: the snow globe, and the mailbox." Her expression softened. "I remember Daisy."

"Daisy." Probably everyone would always remember Daisy. *She was a special woman.* "She was the one who took over the Christmas planning and the festival after my mom." It was still hard to think about those times. The old familiar anxiety twisted in his gut. "Let's go get these wreaths hung."

He walked over to a stack of wreaths. Only eight. Not too bad. Next to them was a planogram of where the ladies wanted the wreaths to be hung. Kevin handed Lisa two wreaths to carry, then picked up the rest of them. "The sooner we get all these hung, then the sooner we can get back to the store and get on with our lives."

"Sure." Lisa led the way back up the wooden staircase. "When we're done, I just need to make one more stop, if you don't mind."

"Okay. No problem. This shouldn't take too long." He liked her spirit. She seemed to be always planning the next steps she needed to take, and unlike so many people he worked with, she wasn't looking to take a break.

Kevin eyed her as they walked out to hang the wreaths, wondering what else she needed to do this morning. He hoped she wasn't one of those people that would be wanting to run back to the hardware store for supplies every day. He'd much rather start a list and do that all at once.

As if she read his mind, she explained. "I need to stop at the inn."

"No problem."

They were done hanging all eight wreaths in less than an hour. As soon as they finished hanging the wreaths, Kevin drove Lisa back over to the inn.

Michelle stepped through the front door of Barbara's Country inn with a stack of cookie decorating supplies in her arms. The smell of fresh cookies filled the air.

"Knock, knock! Megan? I'm here to help with the—" Michelle walked into the kitchen to find David, Thomas and Hannah already gathered around kitchen island helping decorate cookies. "This is a nice surprise."

Thomas nodded. "It is. Hi, Michelle."

"Hi, everyone." Michelle put her coat down and found a place at the island. "I didn't know that you were helping out, too."

"We're keeping up the town tradition," Megan said. "Pitching in on baking cookies for the festival."

Michelle let out a laugh. "Oh, you don't have to tell me about how many cookies we need. I ran this festival last year. I about had a panic attack over trying to get it all pulled together."

"Plus, the ladies in charge of the food were snowed in," Hannah added.

"Don't remind me." Michelle shook her head. Thank goodness it had all turned out wonderfully in the end. She wasn't sad not to be the one running it this year, though.

Megan said, "Barbara told me to offer up the kitchen and pitch in however we could. So, when Hannah told me how many cookies she'd been assigned to make for the festival I told her we should make them here. So here we are."

"And I brought helpers," Hannah said.

David sat at the end of the island, meticulously decorating cookies. "I've done ten elves already! This is Donner, Blitzen, Dasher and—"

"Wait a second." Hannah walked over and looked at the cookies. "Aren't those reindeer names?"

"Yep. I like to keep Santa on his toes."

"I see." She turned and grabbed a cookie sheet to put in the oven. "Confusion in the North Pole! That's how all the best cartoons start."

Michelle took the only empty chair, which just so happened to be right next to Thomas. "Hello." Just being this close to him made her nerves tingle. It really was too bad he was only in town for the holidays. It would be nice to meet someone like him who lived here.

"Hey there." His smile lingered. "Glad to see you again so soon."

She tried to keep her cool, happy to have cookies to

focus on. Her hand shook slightly. Why did he make her so nervous, in a schoolgirl sort of way? Thankfully, Lisa and Kevin walked in at that moment.

"What's going on here?" Lisa stopped at the table to examine all of the gooey frosting and gorgeous baked cookies the decorating party had already produced. "Wow, look at these. It smells so good in here."

"My secret recipe," Hannah said. "My grandmother taught me how to bake these when I still had to stand on a stool to reach the counter."

Kevin stepped behind David and put his hands on the boy's shoulders. "That's a lot of cookies."

"Want to help us?" David asked.

"I don't think we have time."

"Well, actually," Lisa said. "I have to ask you a question, Megan, but Kevin here I'm sure would like to help decorate."

Kevin dropped his head to his chest, laughing. "Sure." He peeled out of his coat and slid between David and Hannah.

Michelle picked up the cookie Thomas had just finished decorating. "I like your crown." She wasn't totally sure if that's what it was, but it was her best guess.

"Ah." He turned the cookie the other way around. "That's... a reindeer."

She'd have never guessed that in a million years. She looked at the cookie again. "Oh. A reindeer. Okay." She didn't want to hurt his feelings, but he took it well.

"No, no, I'm genuinely terrible at decorating cookies." He didn't even seem to mind that he was bad at it, which was kind of refreshing. Some guys couldn't admit a mistake or a shortcoming, no matter how small. She'd dated enough of those types of guys.

At least Thomas was giving it his best effort, and his son sure seemed to be enjoying it. If being bad at decorating cookies was one of his flaws, she could certainly deal with that.

In the foyer, Lisa and Megan stood near the box of Christmas decorations that were still on the foyer table.

"It'd be just for a few days," Lisa explained. "I just want the store to have some Christmas decorations, you know? So what I'd do is I'd put these in the garlands around the door."

"I have a lot of them, so you're welcome to take some." Megan seemed tickled to be included as she handed Lisa the box of ornaments.

"I'll take good care of them and return them as soon as we're done."

"I'm not worried about that. I have plenty of them around. I'm glad they'll be put to good use.

"Thank you so much." Lisa carried the box back to the kitchen. "These are going to look so beautiful. It'll make a huge difference."

"You're welcome."

As they headed back toward the kitchen, laughter

flowed out into the hall. Lisa turned to Megan. "I think they're having fun in here without us."

"Sounds that way." Megan followed the joyful noise back into the kitchen.

Lisa held the big holiday box of ornaments in her arms. "Okay. I'm ready to go."

"Okay." Kevin put down his hand-decorated cookie. "Ready to head back?"

David tilted his head up to the two of them. "Why would you do that?"

Kevin wiped his hands clean. "We've still got a lot of decorating and painting to do."

David eyed them suspiciously. "Isn't frosting cookies just like painting and decorating rolled into one?"

The kid has a point.

Everyone laughed.

"That's my boy," Thomas said with pride.

"I think he's gotcha there," Lisa said to Kevin.

Kevin looked over at David's decorated cookie. He smiled, checked his watch, and agreed. "Yeah, sure. All right. Fine. We'll do three cookies each, then we head out of here."

"Deal." Lisa set the box of ornaments on the counter, and then pulled up a seat.

David beamed. "Awesome." He lifted a green piping bag and added holly to the hat of another elf cookie.

Kevin sat back down next to Lisa, gently bumping her shoulder with his as he got back to work.

Michelle shook red sprinkles onto a bell-shaped ornament. "So, how are you enjoying Evergreen?" she asked Thomas.

"It's...very homey," Thomas said, looking relaxed.

"Well, you know Evergreen has a way of keeping people in town. Mostly." She gave Kevin a pointed look.

Kevin stammered. "Hey, I go where the work is."

"Don't I know it," Thomas said. "I've been trying to get him for years to come work on my operation on my logging site in Maine."

Lisa jerked her head toward Kevin. "Maine, huh?"

"Yeah. I'm thinking about it," he said.

Michelle noticed the passing look on Lisa's face. One of disappointment, maybe.

"I've got some expanding to do. Trying to get a traveling man to settle into a permanent post is proving to be quite tricky."

Kevin lifted his cookie to add dragées to it. "I promise I'll let you know soon."

Thomas nodded like he'd heard that before. "Mmhmm."

Michelle tried to lighten the moment for Lisa. "What about you, Lisa? Where's home?"

"I was a military kid, so we moved around a lot. I guess that's why I'm on the go all the time. I have a place in Boston, but I travel quite a bit for work and...I don't know. I haven't really connected to a place that I love yet. Not since I was a kid."

Not since Evergreen. Michelle would put her money on it.

Kevin held his Christmas tree-shaped sugar cookie up for Lisa to see. He'd iced it with green frosting, then put a gold sprinkle star at the top. Golden garland zigzagged from top to bottom, with silver dragées for ornaments very precisely spaced on the branches. It was actually one of the best ones on the table.

"Wow," Lisa said.

Kevin looked proud. "Any job worth doing is worth doing well." He placed his cookie next to Lisa's. Same shape, but very different decorating styles, Michelle noticed. Lisa's were good, but Kevin's was precise. Which didn't surprise Michelle at all.

He teased Lisa with a little lift of his brows and a smile as he started to decorate his second cookie in exactly the same manner.

Hannah and Megan swapped cookie sheets in and out of the oven, and Michelle and Thomas teamed up on their decorating. He held the cookies and she frosted and shook sprinkles on them, which was bringing much better results for him.

The table was filling up with Christmas trees, snowmen, wreaths and all shapes of sugar cookies and gingerbread men, too. With each cookie, they were all starting to conquer the art of squeezing frosting through the pastry bag. Hannah picked up two matching sugar cookies in the shape of ornaments that she'd just finished and held them up like earrings. David danced his reindeer-named elves across the table in a lighthearted line dance that had everyone laughing.

Thomas decided he was ready to try decorating another cookie on his own, so Michelle let him have at it. He moved slow and methodically, taking time to spread a thin base layer of frosting first, then adding the details.

A couple minutes later he lifted a cookie that looked more like a blob dripping with frosting, jimmies, sprinkles, and candy-coated chocolates down the front. "How about this?" he asked, looking for Michelle's approval.

She took a deep breath. After the "crown" incident she was almost afraid to guess. At least now she had the advantage of knowing which cookie cutters they were using. She eyed it closer, not wanting to embarrass him. The three candy-coated chocolates down the center might be buttons, but that white blob at the top of the hat was the giveaway. "That *is* supposed to be an elf, right?"

"Yes!" Thomas clearly considered that a win. He almost seemed about to take a victory lap.

She reached over to inspect the over-decorated cookie a little closer, and their hands touched. Her heart jumped, and a chill chased through her. Did he notice it, too?

He received a round of applause for his improvement on this cookie from the others, while her heart applauded his touch. Hopefully the clapping and cheering was enough of a distraction for her to pull herself together before anyone else noticed.

"Thank you very much," Thomas said beaming. "Thank you. Success."

Kevin's phone beeped. He pulled it out of his pocket to read the text message. "Oh. Hey. The guy has the beam up and secured at Daisy's," he announced. "I think we're all set. We should get back, Lisa."

"All right. Great." Lisa handed the cookie she was frosting to David. "Finish that up for me, will you?"

"Sure."

"And stop by the store to try out all the locks there later," she suggested.

"Don't worry, we will," Hannah said. "We're running out of places to check."

Michelle was grateful to be a part of this group today. That little spark between Lisa and Kevin seemed to be contagious. She was feeling the same with Thomas. Funny that she'd known Hannah for so long and never met him before. *Timing is everything.*

Chapter Eight

Kevin drove back to the town square. With the garland and lights up on the front of the store and the red bench moved back outside to the porch, even from the street Daisy's looked cheerier already. He parallel parked along the curb right in front of the store.

"You straightened and secured the store sign," Lisa said. "When did you do that?"

"This morning before I picked you up."

"You *are* an early bird. It looks wonderful. Thank you." Lisa grabbed the box of ornaments and jumped out of the truck, still eyeing the sign. "I love it."

He exhaled a long sigh of contentment. "This has already been a great day."

A sunny cheerfulness filled her as she went to unlock the front door with a bounce in her step.

Kevin got his toolbox out of the back of the truck while Lisa worked the key in the old lock and pushed it open, holding it for him. "After you."

He made a beeline for the beam. Just the fact that there wasn't one lying diagonally across the space opened it up. He looked up. "All right. They did a nice job. A coat of paint and that will be like new."

"They did. It looks great." Lisa spread her arms out as she walked through the clear room. "It feels so much bigger."

"That's terrific, I'll—" As soon as he lowered his focus, he noticed the place on the wall where the damage had left its mark. "Oh, no."

"Hmm." Lisa followed him closer to the damage. "It's not that bad. We can just cover it up with some plywood, and a couple coats of paint." She shrugged. "No big deal."

He shot her a cold look. "It could be damaged on the inside," he said abruptly. He kneeled down, inspecting it closer. "Maybe even the pipes." This was exactly what he'd been afraid of. Unforeseen issues. He'd been on enough jobs where sloppy work had covered up problems resulting in impossible deadlines, project overruns, or worse...someone getting hurt. "No. This is a big deal."

She swiveled slowly. "I suppose that means you want to open up that wall."

"Yep. Wouldn't you?"

Lisa looked at the wall and back at him. "Well, yeah, we can't risk there being water damage in there, but—"

"It's going to add some labor. We might have to bring in a plumber."

"Do we have time for that?"

Kevin turned on her. Sacrificing good craftsmanship for the timeline was a mistake. "If a pipe bursts, it would take twice as long and cost twice as much." He stood, trying to contain his frustration, but this was a sore subject for him.

"I know. I'm agreeing with you." She cowered back a little. "I'm not saying we cut corners—"

"Aren't you?"

"No. I'm—"

"It seems like you are."

Behind them, the bell to the door tinkled and Ezra walked in. "Wow. This looks a lot better." He looked pleased as he walked around with a broad smile of approval.

Lisa glanced over at Kevin, then smiled and somehow managed a perky lilt to her voice. "We're not done yet, but—"

Ezra pressed his palms together in front of him. "You see, that's just what I wanted to see you about." His expression stilled and grew serious. "I know you had a few more days before you were ready, but the buyer called today and she said she can only look at the place tomorrow."

Lisa shrank back.

"Tomorrow?" Kevin came flying around the counter. "No. Ezra. There are repairs we've got to take care of before we can even think about—"

"I think we can." Lisa's voice was soft, but her position firm as she held his stare.

A little bewildered, Ezra looked back and forth between the two.

Kevin stepped in closer to Lisa. "Look. I appreciate the enthusiasm, I do, but I just don't see how we can." His jaw pulsed.

Lisa took a deep breath, and her eyes filled with determination. Without her normal cheerfulness, she calmly leveled a stare, and said, "I don't see how we can't try."

Kevin didn't like it one bit. He wasn't covering up potential problems no matter what. She wasn't going to give in, though, and what choice did they have? An early buyer was still a buyer. Giving it a try only meant starting to do what needed to be done anyway. Clearing his throat, he said the words slowly as if testing out the idea. "All right. Fine. Let's see what we can do."

Ezra seemed a little confused by their altercation, but instantly relieved. "I appreciate it." He got out of there as fast as he could, as if he feared they might change their minds.

Lisa faced Kevin. Very matter-of-factly, she said, "So, if you just want to start on the wall, I'll get started on the shelves." She took off her coat and walked over to the other side of the room.

He hadn't meant to blow up on her. He took his coat off and grabbed the broom that was leaning against the counter. It was going to be a long night if they weren't going to talk. He started to sweep the sawdust from the floor. She quietly cleaned the shelves. The absence of her bubbly good nature was deafening.

Unable to stand the quiet between them, he reached over and pushed the power button on the radio.

Christmas music echoed through the space.

Lisa stood across the room in her soft pink sweater, wiping down shelves. She turned to him for a moment, then looked away and concentrated on the task at hand. Once she finished cleaning the shelves, she put down her rag and walked to the corner of the room.

She got out her phone, and he heard her side of the conversation.

"Hi, Hannah. It's Lisa. I hope I'm not catching you at a bad time."

A pause.

"Ezra stopped by. The buyer is coming tomorrow. Is there any way I can get you and Michelle to come over and help me get things together here at the store in the morning?" He could hear the hope in her voice.

"You don't know how much this means to me. Is eight-thirty too early? There's so much to do... Thank you so much. I'll see you then."

Lisa hung up the phone and let out a sigh. For two hours the music filled the space and they kept working, crossing things off the list as quickly as they could.

Kevin installed the wainscoting he'd painted to cover the front counter on the left side of the store. Rather than let the scraps go to waste, he had just enough to also install it beneath the windows on the front wall. It gave the place an immediate facelift.

Lisa finished cleaning the shelves, then lined the glass front counter on the righthand side of the store with a layer of white fleece, making it look like snow. She'd staggered some Christmas decorations. It wasn't much, but it somehow made that side of the store appear fuller.

"I think we should call it a night," he said. "If you want, I can take you to get the Christmas tree from Dad's first thing."

She hesitated, but finally nodded. "That would be great. It'll have to be early. Hannah and the gang are going to meet me here at eight-thirty in the morning to help me arrange whatever we've got. I sure hope this works."

He looked around. "It already looks brighter. With some merchandise it will be even more eye-appealing."

She shrugged. "All we can do is try."

"Let me give you a ride back to the inn."

She put down her rag, and he was afraid for a second that she was going to turn down his offer, opting to walk rather than be alone with him in the truck.

"Look. I'm sorry I blew up on you." He lowered his head. "Shortcuts can be dangerous. People can get hurt. I overreacted. I just want to do the right thing." He didn't need to tell her the whole story, but he'd learned his lesson about shortcuts, and no one would make him compromise on his standards. It was his reputation at stake.

She started to say something, then stopped.

"I really am sorry. It won't happen again." He reached his hand out.

From across the room she walked toward him. The radio played "Silver Bells."

"Forgive me?" He took her hand and spun her in the middle of the wide-open store. "Please?" In a couple days this place might belong to someone else, and she'd be heading off to Boston or to wherever her next job took her. He didn't want to miss the chance to dance with her even for just one spin here at Daisy's.

She laughed when he pulled her to him and swayed, and then relaxed into his arms. "I do understand about the shortcuts. It's just—"

"I understand your point too. It never hurts to try." He twirled her, then pulled her hands into his chest.

She spoke softly. "You're full of surprises."

They swayed to the music. "So do you forgive me?"

"I do."

He hadn't meant to snap at her. He'd overreacted, and he'd hurt her feelings. That bothered him. More than it should, maybe. He held her hand tight, not really wanting to let go. She felt nice in his arms, and she let him lead. They danced until the end of the song.

"Ready to go?" He asked with a nod, half-hoping she'd say no.

"Not really, but we should."

His racing heart knew exactly how she felt.

Chapter Nine

The next morning, Lisa struggled with conflicting thoughts about Kevin. His short temper had been unexpected. He was passionate about his work, but the way he'd come at her about the repairs had been unsettling. Still, she understood where he was coming from. She was passionate about her work and her reputation, too.

Then there'd been the apology, and dancing. The dancing had been totally unexpected. And nice.

Just thinking about it made her insides twirl.

She stood at the door with her coat on her arm and a mug of coffee in her hand, waiting on him. She checked her watch. He should be here any time now. She put her coffee down, put on her coat, and patted her coat pocket where the letter from Santa still lay tucked safely inside.

It was hard to believe that letter had been lost all those years, and then turned up just like that. What were the odds of it being a letter from someone who was working on the store at the time it was found? That seemed like a lot more than a coincidence to her.

She wondered if Kevin would remember writing that letter. She remembered the last letter she mailed to Santa at Daisy's, word for word.

She needed to tell him about the letter, but after last night, she was a little nervous to do so. It was personal. She wasn't so sure she'd appreciate someone reading something from her past.

He pulled up in front of the inn.

I'll tell him today.

She raced out the door with her coffee.

"Good morning," he said with a smile as she opened the door and got in.

"Good morning." She buckled her seat belt, and as Kevin backed out of the driveway, she wondered how she might slip that old Santa letter into conversation at some point. It would be a little weird to just blurt it out right now.

Evergreen had been blanketed with fresh snow again overnight, making everything seem fresh and clean. They rode through town and then to the state road that led to the outskirts of town where the roads got hillier and more winding. The limbs drooped over, heavy with snow.

"We made good progress last night," he said.

"We did. This morning will make all the difference."

"The merchandise?"

"And the tree," she said.

"Do you know what kind of tree you like best?"

"Douglas firs," Lisa said without hesitation. "They're softer."

"But they're sorta big and round. They're like a potato-shaped tree."

Clearly not his favorite. Lisa laughed and Kevin joined her. "Okay, so they need more trimming, yes. Granted. But they're softer. Children can touch a Douglas fir—they're a good indoor tree." Would she ever be able to decorate a Douglas fir again without thinking of it looking like a Mr. Potato Head?

"Hmm."

She eyed him with smug delight. "Well then. What's your favorite?"

Kevin turned and leveled a stare as if he knew he'd get an argument from her. "Fraser fir."

"Really?"

"They smell great, and have great needle retention."

"Mr. Practical." She puckered her lips. "True. But it won't be up that long, so needle retention won't be that big of a deal."

"Plus, they are sturdy enough to hold ornaments. And I like the bluish-green color." He raised his shoulders. "It was always my mom's favorite tree."

Her heart wrenched as she looked over at him. That was so sweet. She couldn't imagine losing her mother at such a young age. That had to have been so hard. "Maybe we could have one of each."

Then, at the risk of starting another argument, she added, "I still say we need a tree indoor and outdoor."

"And I still say that's too many trees." He kept his

eyes on the road. "Look, if we get overly ambitious, we run out of time, and one of them just ends up looking sloppy."

"Sloppy. Mmm." But he didn't know how good she was at this. She decorated trees in half the time of anyone else and could still make it look like a million bucks. *Pick your battles.* "Good point."

Kevin took a right onto a snowy dirt road. The tires crunched as they followed the ruts along the snow-covered lane that led back to a big, shiny red barn. Kevin glanced up the hill on the right.

Lisa followed his line of sight and her gaze landed on an old farmhouse. He'd probably grown up there.

He veered to the left toward the equipment sheds, an old wooden and concrete dairy barn and a bright red, brand new one. "Nice barn."

"Dad had it built just a little over a year ago. The town used it for the Christmas Eve festival last year when town hall got flooded at the last minute."

She shuddered inwardly. "I bet that was a near catastrophe."

"I wasn't here, but I heard all about it."

Kevin whipped the old '56 Ford around in front of dozens and dozens of Christmas trees lined up against a two-by-four stockade, like frozen soldiers ready for duty.

The barn had sliding doors—the kind with white x's on them. Above them hung a painted sign that read "Henry's Christmas Tree Lot" in fun lettering, surrounded by snowflakes and presents.

Lisa pointed at the picturesque metal windmill that stood in the field just beyond the Christmas trees. "I love that."

"Oh, yeah. That's been here for longer than I've been alive."

"They are so cool. I just love the way they look."

"Back in the day they were common as a good pair of jeans. It still works. It fills the stock tank with water, but when dad was a kid that was their water source."

"Wow. I love that. You know, feeling connected to the past like that."

"I guess so. I hadn't really thought about it like that." He nodded toward an old building that had seen better days. "Nothing goes to waste on a farm. That was the original barn. Now Dad uses it as the sales stand for the wreaths and trees, and a place to trim and wrap the trees for transport."

Kevin pulled the truck up next to the smaller building. Across the way, a man got off an old blue Ford tractor that produced a loud throaty clatter even at idle. He pulled off his work gloves as he made his way toward them.

They got out of the truck. The smell of diesel hung in the air.

"Hey, Dad," Kevin said. "This is Lisa."

"Lisa!" Henry smiled and threw his arms wide. "A town this small, you can't keep anything very quiet. Nice to meet you."

"It's nice to meet you, Mr. Miller."

"Call me Henry."

"Okay. Henry." She pushed her hands into the pockets of her puffy coat. "Well, Henry, you have a gorgeous new barn."

"Why thank you." He turned and walked toward the tree building. "My wife Ruth and I use to run the whole farm singlehandedly from this table right here in this old barn."

"Yeah?" That must have been neat. That explained why the old building was still being used, too.

Kevin hung back. As they got to the sales counter, Lisa noticed something sitting on the table between an old-style metal cash box and a basket of fruit. "Oh, look at this old Underwood typewriter."

Henry let out a hearty laugh. "Kevin used to pound away on this thing when he was just a kid. Despite it not working properly."

Kevin walked over and tapped on the keys. "These old typewriters make such great noise." He pushed the platen to the end, making the bell ding.

"Yeah." Maybe this would be a good segue to mention the letter to Santa. But Kevin seemed quiet— almost shy or nervous around his dad. The timing seemed wrong. She'd have to wait. "Okay, Henry, we need a Fraser fir."

Kevin turned to her with satisfaction on his face. She returned the smile.

"You're in luck." Henry pulled on his gloves. "I ordered too many of those. Come right this way."

They walked down the lot toward the long rows of trees.

"So, you're busy putting Daisy's shop back together?"

"Your son here is doing all the work. I just stand around looking bossy. You should stop by sometime."

"Ah, yeah." Henry glanced at Kevin, then waved a hand toward the farm. "I'm pretty busy here, and umm…"

Kevin looked over at his dad, who paused, a quiet moment hanging between them. Strands of lights with those old Edison bulbs were strung from one end of the lot to the other. They cast an interesting glow in the grey morning.

Henry dipped his head and turned and walked away. "The trees are right over here." His smile was tight.

Awkwardly, Kevin cleared his throat, then shrugged his shoulders in mock resignation. She wondered if things had always been so tense between the two of them.

"You coming?" Henry called out from behind the building.

"Yes." Lisa and Kevin hurried to catch up.

Lisa eyed the Douglas firs as they passed by them, but when Henry pointed out the Fraser he had in mind for Daisy's, she knew it was perfect. It was tall and wide and the fragrance hit her when she got close. "I love it."

"Are you sure?" Kevin didn't seem to agree.

"Yes. It'll fit perfectly outside the store."

A couple of young guys untied the tree from the

boards and carried it over to the truck. Henry lifted the big tree over the back of the tailgate. With Kevin on the passenger rail and her on the driver's, she watched Kevin lay the tree down.

"It's perfect," she said. "Thank you."

"I don't know about perfect," Kevin said. "It has a bare spot on one side."

"Some of them do." Henry's words were clipped. "That's just how trees are. You just put the bald spot in the corner."

Kevin put a red strap across the tree and handed the other end to Lisa, who ran the end of the strap through the side rail and passed the strap back over to Kevin.

"There is no corner," Kevin said. "We're putting it in front of—"

"We can just put it up against a wall," she offered.

Henry shook his head, a little stern.

"Son, you have the best eye of anyone I know. Makes you a great contractor. But sometimes, you've just got to slow down."

Lisa frowned. What was that about?

Kevin looked at the tree with a grimace. "It's fine." She could tell he just wanted out of this conversation.

It was awkward watching this unfold between the two men. She wished there was something she could do or say to make things better. But she knew there wasn't. Whatever was simmering between these two had been brewing for a long time.

For a long, painful moment, she stood there, and

then finally stepped down from the truck sideboard, walked around to the passenger side, and got in.

She watched Kevin go and settle up with his dad, and then she pretended to be checking emails on her phone when he got back. Why had he insisted on coming here to his dad's lot if it was going to be so uncomfortable? Families could be so complicated.

"All set," he said, with a tap on the steering wheel. "Let's get this tree back to Daisy's."

She was relieved when he turned on the radio, even if it was a scratchy AM station. At least the Christmas music would dull the silence. They drove back to Daisy's and unloaded the tree.

Kevin steadied it on its base. "Where do you want it?"

Lisa turned, a finger to her lips, and eyed the front of the store. "Let's put it on the righthand side of the porch. Right in the center of the corner beam there."

With a grunt he lifted the tree and moved in that direction.

"I can help carry it," she said, running alongside him.

"I've got it. You want to go get the tree stand?"

"Yes. I'm on it." She ran inside the store, frantically trying to remember where she'd last seen it. Finally, she found it on the floor of the stock room and went back outside. "I've got it," she said, holding it over her head. She squatted and placed it right where she wanted it.

Kevin set the tree in the stand, and Lisa tightened

the screws. "It should stand on its own now. Do you want to see if it's straight?"

He let go, and the tree stood. He walked out to the street and closed one eye, checking it against the straight line of the front post. "It's dead on."

"Awesome!" She gave each of the screws one extra twist for good measure.

"It'll need lots of water the first few days."

"No problem. I've got a watering can I was going to use for decoration. Now it can earn its keep. I'll get some water and the rest of the magnolia flowers." She raised her hands like a director might block a scene. "We'll just tuck them sporadically in the branches of the tree. It'll tie the garland, storefront and tree all together. It's going to be great." She thought of the bare spot on the tree. No one would ever see it against the wall. Perfect enough. Just enough off-kilter. That thought satisfied her.

She walked inside to get some water. Kevin followed her. "I'll get the step stool."

"Okay." She gave him a smile. As he walked back by, she tossed him the near-empty box of magnolias and pine cones that were left over from putting up the garland. He caught it with one hand and a winning smile, then went back outside.

After she watered the tree, she walked back inside to go through the stockpile of ornaments in the back room. She found some that would work perfectly with her design scheme, and even came across some things to spruce up the inside of the store. There were a few Santas and seven different wreaths, including a grapevine wreath with holly berries and pinecones, and one made out of cottonseed pods. Behind the wreaths there were three large boxes labelled "Nutcrackers," "Stockings," "Sleighs." If those were really the contents, she was in good shape. She carefully pulled the tape back on the first one. Just as it said on the box in bold magic marker, it was a box full of different nutcrackers.

Tucked in the side of the box was a long string of lights. She quickly plugged them in to see if they worked. To her delight, they lit up and sparkled. She tugged them out of the box and wrapped the long strand around her arm in a loop.

Yes. Things are starting to come together.

With a box of ornaments in her arms, she grabbed an extension cord on the way outside to see how Kevin was doing with the tree.

Kevin had already placed the pinecones and magnolia flowers on the tree, and they were perfectly haphazard. Just the way she liked them.

"We're in luck," she said. "I found these in the back with the ornaments." She carried the long strand of tiny white tree lights over to Kevin. "Here you go." He took them, and she stood there for a second. "I've got more work to do inside unless you need me to—"

"No, no. I've got this. We're going to be pressed for time as it is."

Time. Always worried about time. She wished he'd lighten up.

"I just hope these work," he grumbled.

She took the end and plugged it into the extension cord. "Watch this." They all lit up. "Ta-da. Magic."

He smiled wide. "Nicely done."

She unplugged the lights, laughing. "Here. Let me help you with this. It can get a little tricky." They wrapped the lights around the tree, handing the loop of wire back and forth between them. It somehow felt natural to work with him, despite the friction between them other day. Everyone had conflicts sometimes.

"So...your dad," she ventured.

"Yeah." He looked a little embarrassed. "We, uh...I spent a lot of time *not* coming home for Christmas. It's just never been the same without my mom. For either one of us. We avoided it for a long time, but... my dad's getting older. So for the past couple of years I've been trying to come home. Trying to be here." He handed the light strand back to her.

"And how's that been coming along?"

A nervous laugh escaped. "We can get...father and son about things, you know. I was just gone for so long, and we each have this idea of who the other one is, y'know?"

"Yeah. I do know." Lisa nodded. "Everyone keeps telling me they wish I'd put down some roots. That's all I ever hear. But we moved around a lot when I was a kid. I guess that's really what I'm used to."

He became animated. "Plus, it's great to travel for work."

"Right," Lisa said, happy to know she wasn't the only one who loved that.

"New cities. New people."

Lisa waved her hands in the air. "Yeah, you get to try out all the best burgers in any given town."

"Right! I do that all the time," he said.

"You too?" It was funny how many things they had in common.

"Oops." Kevin tugged on the lights. "We have a snag."

She gently lifted the lights to free them from where they'd tangled between the branches of the tree. "There you go." She arranged them on her side and then handed them back to him around the back of the tree.

"Hang on. I've got another snag." He pulled on the strand, then stretched the end toward her. "Grab this."

"I've got it on this side." She closed her hand expecting the lights and getting his hand, which gave her butterflies like crazy. She sucked in a breath. When she leaned back to look, Kevin was smiling at their hands. He felt it too.

"Thanks." She moved the lights into place trying to slow down her pounding heart. Something just shifted in their relationship. She could tell by the look in his eyes.

Chapter Ten

Kevin hadn't felt this way in a long time. Lisa had a way of letting him lower his guard. He rubbed his fingers together, still feeling the spark of when their hands met. It had been a while since he'd dated anyone, but he couldn't remember the last time a woman left him feeling like this. A little frantic, off-balance. The natural, undeniable attraction was only the start of it. There was the good work they were sharing, too. And her passion for her work matched his. A first, for sure.

Trying to pull himself together, his eyes wandered across the street where Michelle, Thomas, Hannah and David were standing outside of the Home Bakery next door to the Kringle Kitchen.

David was probably still trying that mystery key out on doors. Hannah was a good aunt to let that kid drag her around. There was nothing that gave any indication whatsoever that the key even went to anything in this town. It could've come from anywhere. For that matter, it could've been purely decorative.

He heard them talking from across the street.

"It doesn't fit. How about Daisy's store?" David pointed right at him.

"That's a great idea," said Hannah.

David took off in a run, dragging Hannah along by the arm. Thomas and Michelle were catching up with them just as David struggled with the key on Daisy's door.

"Hey guys," Hannah said.

"Hey!" Lisa peered around the tree.

"We were just trying the key on Daisy's store, and it's not working," Hannah said.

David looked disappointed. Hannah gave him a squeeze. "We'll keep trying later," she said. "I know we're early, Lisa, but it looks like you could use some help now."

"Yes, I wasn't expecting you until eight-thirty, but I sure could use the help." Lisa stepped away from the tree. "You can help Kevin with this," she said to Thomas and David. Gesturing to Hannah and Michelle to follow her, she said, "I have to go inside and finish up the decorations."

"Dad, can you help me?" David asked, grabbing the handmade tree topper, a top hat with a magnolia and a pretty feather spray of pine and holly on it. "I want to put the tree topper on."

As Lisa, Hannah and Michelle headed toward the store, Thomas picked up David. "One. Two. Three. Oh wow, you are getting way too big for this."

"Seriously too big," David agreed, laughing as his dad set him down.

Kevin looked on at Thomas and David's relationship. He'd once been that close with his dad, too. Things had gotten so off track between the two of them. He'd been about David's age when Mom died. He hadn't known how to deal with his own feelings, and seeing Dad so hurt still felt like an open wound when he let himself think about it.

Dad had become a very different man after that. Closed off, and angry. Now he understood more what his father had gone through, but the damage between them had already been done.

Thomas looked over at him. "Kevin, I've been thinking through a few things and wanted to run something by you."

"Sure. What's up?"

"It's about work." It probably had to do with the job offer. Hopefully he hadn't waited too long to give him an answer that he'd filled the position with another candidate. He had his attention now. It was time to make a decision. "Okay."

"Okay. First things first. Let's finish this tree." Thomas handed a gold ball to Kevin that David had just put a hook on. The three of them made an assembly line, cutting down dramatically on the time it would've taken to finish decorating the tree.

When they were done, Kevin stepped back.

"It looks great," said David. He high-fived his dad.

Kevin had to admit Dad had been right. This was

a nice tree, and no one would ever notice the bad spot. *Sorry, Dad. Sorry for reacting so negatively.* He needed to tell him how nice the tree looked when he saw him later.

With Kevin, Thomas, and David handling the outside, Lisa got down to business inside the store. Michelle, Lisa, and Hannah draped the store with garlands and hung Megan's ornaments carefully between the evergreens. The space was coming together so nicely.

She handed Hannah the box labeled "Nutcrackers." "I don't know exactly how many are in there, but you can use them to fill the shelves behind the counter over there. Spread them out. Maybe mix them in with some of the little things already around."

"Got it."

Lisa handed the next box off to Michelle. "This box has stockings and an adorable garland made of miniature stockings. There's all kinds of cute stuff like that in here. Go wild. Use it to brighten up the place."

"This will be fun." Michelle grabbed the box and headed for the counter, rummaging through it as she did. "Oh, you're right. This stocking garland is great. I love how colorful it is. I hope there's enough of it to drape across the whole back shelving unit. Wouldn't that be cute?"

"It would." Lisa took the wreaths and hung them around the store, then got the stepladder and started hanging ornaments from wide red ribbon at different lengths in the front display windows. Daisy had always used shimmery metallic ribbon, but this would be festive and eye-catching, and hopefully tickle a few memories in the townsfolk that used to frequent the store.

She hung fifteen in each window, for no specific reason except that it was her favorite number, then stepped down from the ladder to see how it looked. She turned to the girls. "What do you think?"

Hannah and Michelle both nodded their approval as they continued to unpack and arrange items. "I like it," Hannah said.

"It reminds me of what Daisy used to put up in the windows."

"Yes!" Lisa was so excited. "That's exactly what I was going for. That's how I remembered it too. Not exactly, but similar."

Lisa walked outside. The windows still looked a little bare. Probably because there wasn't that much going on inside. The display needed a little something more.

She walked back inside, got paper and scissors, and started cutting out snowflakes. Some even looked a little like daisies. With a dozen different ones in front of her—all different sizes—she finally pulled five aside. She took a thin piece of cardboard from the bottom of one of the empty boxes and traced the snowflake patterns on the cardboard, then cut them out. Some large and some small. With the flocking in hand, she carefully spritzed the templates against the glass, leaving the cutest white snowy snowflake pattern behind. Fifteen minutes later she had a Christmas tree made of snow-flocked, daisy-shaped snowflakes in each of the front windows.

Michelle came around the corner. "Lisa, you are amazing. It's hard to believe this is the same place we were standing in just a few days ago."

"I can't imagine what the real stores look like after you work your magic," Hannah said.

"Thanks." She picked up a crate of decorations and carried them to the counter. "If I had time, I would have staged the whole store," Lisa said. "Put real product on the shelves, made it seem like an actual functioning store."

"Everything out front is done." Kevin walked in with Thomas and David right behind him.

"Fabulous." Lisa spun around to David. "How's it look?"

"Like Santa's elves came and did the job themselves."

"That's really good," Lisa said. She'd just finished lining up old pop bottles and collectibles inside the apothecary they'd painted with a fresh coat of white paint. "Kevin, could you hang some lights around this to make it more of a focal point?"

"I can do that."

The shelves were beginning to look better. Some of the things were random, like someone's old wedding bouquet and even some bottles that looked far from collectible, but at least they looked uniform and gave the shelf a sense of fullness.

"Oh!" Lisa spun around toward Hannah. "Do you have that pine spray stuff I gave you?"

"Yes. Right here." Hannah started spritzing it into the air.

The bells on the front door jingled against the glass. Ezra walked in with a woman wearing a white cashmere coat and carrying a designer bag. She looked so polished. Lisa almost hated for her to walk through the store, lest she get dirty.

"Hi," the woman said. "Don't mind us. We're just stopping in."

"Hello, everyone." Ezra looked like a scared rabbit. "This is—"

"Nancy Redinger." The woman looked at the place with not so much disdain as concern. "It's so good to meet you."

Ezra motioned behind Nancy, mouthing, "Buyer."

"Oh! Hi! Nice to meet you." Lisa stepped over and shook the woman's hand. "You're...just a bit early."

Michelle and Hannah quickly swept a box of decorations under the counter and smiled.

"Yes, and I'm sorry about that, but I wanted to make this decision before first quarter," Nancy explained. "New year, new decisions. You know how it is."

"Right, well—" Lisa started.

A myriad of yesses came from the group with nervous laughter. None of them had ever been in that position, but everyone was rolling with the flow.

Nancy knocked on the counter. "Solid. I like it. Sturdy frame."

Ezra knocked on the counter behind her.

"Center of town location." She glanced around the space. "Mmm. Fresh pine smell," she said with a smile.

Hannah hid the spray bottle behind her back. Lisa gave Ezra a wink. That pine scent had been just in the nick of time.

"We should get out of your way," Lisa said. "Let you take a look and—"

"I'll just be a few minutes. I usually get a sense of these things right away," Nancy said.

Lisa wasn't sure if that was good or bad, but she grabbed her coat, and the others grabbed theirs and raced for the door, too. Just as Lisa was opening it, Nancy climbed the stairs to the back of the store. Ezra turned and gave them a thumbs up.

Lisa, Kevin, Hannah, Michelle, and David all dashed across the street to the Kringle Kitchen.

"All of you together at once?" Carol asked. "What a nice surprise." She motioned them to the large table near the front window.

"The buyer came early." Lisa put her coat on the back of a chair and sat down facing Daisy's Country Store. Kevin sat down next to her.

"Oh dear. I bet that shook Ezra up. He hates surprises," Carol said. "I'll get hot chocolate and cookies. Stand by."

Michelle and Thomas sat on the other side of Lisa. Carol and Joe came back to the table with six cups of hot chocolate and a plate of cookies.

"So she seemed impressed?" Carol asked.

"I wish I'd had more time. She seemed to like it." Lisa leaned forward. "Look. I see them. It looks like she's still deciding. Can anyone read lips?"

Everyone shook their heads.

Nancy and Ezra walked out of the store still talking. They looked up, as if talking about the outside of the building, then Ezra pulled out a clipboard to explain something. Thank goodness Kevin had fixed the sign. It looked a lot better. Lisa nudged Kevin. "She has to see the potential, right?"

"The place is *all* potential," he said.

Lisa's jaw dropped as if insulted.

"I'm kidding." He nudged her back. "We did great."

Lisa reached over and grabbed Kevin's hand—and then realized what she'd done.

He looked down, then gave her hand a squeeze.

Her insides whirled at his touch. Did he feel that too? Chalking it up to a job well done and nothing more, she let go and put her hands under her chin.

"This is so exciting." Carol placed the carafe of hot chocolate on the table. "Nobody can replace Daisy, but—"

"But it'd be nice to bump into each other in the store again," Michelle finished the thought.

"Yes," Carol said dreamily. Joe hugged her shoulder.

"Anything would be better than it becoming a parking lot or something too big and bulky that changes the town forever," Joe said. "It's like that letter said: "What Christmas used to be."

Kevin's brows pulled together. He looked over his shoulder to Joe who was standing behind him. "What letter?"

Oh, dear. Lisa looked over at Kevin.

Michelle spoke up. "Lisa was moving the mailbox, and she found—"

"Yeah, and I was going to mention this to you before." Oh, how she wished she already had. Lisa took the letter from her pocket, and then handed it to Kevin. "I kept wanting to mention this to you, but I found your letter."

"*My* letter?" He took it from her and unfolded it.

"I assumed that it was from when you were a kid." She watched him begin to read it. His hands shook slightly.

"Oh," Carol said with excitement. "Here comes Ezra."

Lisa stood, rubbing her hands together and hoping for good news.

Ezra came in and stopped in the center of the Kringle Kitchen. His jaw tight, he dropped his hands to his sides. "Unfortunately, she's not going to put in an offer."

Lisa's heart sank.

"Did she say why?" Michelle asked.

Ezra shook his head. "She said she loved the store. It just wasn't right for her."

She'd let him down. If I'd only had more time. It was such a wonderful place; how had Nancy Redinger not felt it? Joe and Carol swapped a worried glance.

Sounding as chipper as she could, Lisa said, "But. You still have another buyer, right?"

Kevin stood, still clutching the letter as he read and reread it.

"I'm afraid the other one dropped out. It's just too close to Christmas." Ezra looked crestfallen.

Lisa ached for Ezra, but then Kevin got up to leave. He looked stunned as he reread the letter again over near the Christmas tree.

Her troubled heart twinged. She should've told Kevin about the letter as soon as they'd found it. Now it seemed like she'd been holding out on him. She felt like she'd just exposed his most personal secrets.

She walked over next to Kevin wishing for the right words. She sure had made a mess of things. With Daisy's and now Kevin. "I was waiting for the right time to ask you about it."

"No, I understand," Kevin said. "This is…thank you for this."

"You're welcome." But those words didn't seem nearly enough.

He handed the letter back to her, then pulled on his coat. "I…umm…excuse me."

Kevin left, and Lisa stood there clinging to the letter as he drove off.

A dark heaviness came over her. The disappointment in Ezra and Kevin's faces today was almost too much to bear. And she was responsible for both.

She should've never come back.

Chapter Eleven

*L*isa stepped outside to get some air.

Watching Kevin leave the store with that far-off lost look on his face weighed on her. That and the sound of Ezra's voice as he recounted the visit with Nancy Redinger and her not placing an offer. And what was the common denominator between those things?

Me.

She should've told Kevin sooner. It was too late now. It didn't matter that her intentions had been good. And she shouldn't have promised Ezra she could pull off such a big job in that time frame. This wasn't her first rodeo. Customers got anxious and jumped the gun. It happened all the time on real jobs.

She'd let herself become so focused on her goals and desires that she didn't look at the full effect on everyone around her. Something she'd always said she wouldn't do.

Lisa took her phone out of her pocket and called

her lifeline. Oliver. Through thick and thin, Oliver was always there.

Huddled outside of the Kringle Kitchen in the snow, she waited for him to answer. "Are you busy?"

"Never too busy for you," he said. "What's up?"

She could barely hear him. She wasn't sure if it was the rush of the windy snow on her end or just a bad connection. "It's noisy. Where are you?"

"On a train," he said, not offering any other explanation.

A train? He was probably joking around. Like always. "Alrighty then. If you've got a minute I need your ear."

"I've got all the minutes you need."

She told him about the project staging Daisy's Country Store to help sell it, the potential buyer not biting, and pretty much everything except what was really bothering her. "And I just…maybe it was too big a job for the time I had, but Kevin and I really wanted it to work. And now—"

"Now you'll think of something, because you always do," Oliver reassured her. "So. Cut to the chase and tell me more about this guy you clearly have a crush on."

Lisa stopped mid-stride, nervous energy making her laugh. She dug her free hand deeper into the pocket of her puffy coat.

"Oliver. I don't think I have a cr…I do *not* have a crush. Okay? I mean maybe it's…" She stopped pacing, and let out a breath. *Do I?* "No. I do. I do."

She started pacing again. Partly to keep warm, and partly to help straighten out her thoughts. She always did her best thinking when she paced. *At my age? A crush? Oh my gosh, it's definitely a crush.*

"Oliver, I shouldn't have a crush. I don't live here. He doesn't even live here. I don't even know if he likes me."

"Have you asked him to do something?"

"Maybe it's the season. I'm all caught up in the Christmas of everything." She spun around and walked back.

"Lisa, just ask him to do something with you. Something *not* work-related. If he says yes, then he likes you. If he says no, he probably still likes you."

"Thank you for that very confusing advice, Oliver." She was so frustrated. "I just wish I knew what to do with the store."

"Hang on," Oliver said. "I've got a call... Oh, I should get this. It's Polly."

"Aww. Tell her I said hey." A thought struck. "Wait a minute. Oliver? That's it. You're brilliant!"

"What? I mean, sure, but...what?"

"We need to tell Polly about Daisy's Country Store. It's perfect for her. The location is great, and it really has turned out so nice. We could use a lot of the same ideas we did in her Burlington store in this space. It would look amazing."

"You're right. She said she was going to open a few more stores. This could work for everyone. I'll touch base with you later."

"No! Call or text me right back. Tell her she has to see this store. It's perfect for her. Plus, we'd have fun staging it for her here. You'd love Evergreen. They're getting ready for the big Christmas Eve festival. It's going to be spectacular."

"Christmas Eve festival? Okay. Stand by." Oliver disconnected the call. Lisa did a happy dance right there among the red and white tables on the sidewalk in front of the Kringle Kitchen.

She stole a peek inside at Ezra still talking to the others. His furrowed brows made an underline of the four creases in his forehead. If she could have just one more chance, she knew she could make something good happen for Daisy's Country Store. She wanted this so badly.

Turning to face the store, Daisy's already looked alive again. She crossed her fingers and checked her phone. Not that it was likely that she'd missed the call.

Call back, Oliver.

Time ticked by so slowly.

She silently prayed for help. Not even a miracle, just another shot at giving Daisy's a second chance. *Please.*

Her phone didn't even get a chance to complete the ring before she hit the button. "What did she say? Please tell me she said yes."

Oliver's voice was steady. "Lisa, don't have a heart attack. We've got a lot of work to do."

"With Polly? Is she coming to the store? Or do

you mean just jobs in general? Oliver, tell me what she said!"

"Of course she said she'd come see Daisy's," he said. "No one ever turns me down."

"That is so true. You're right. You're you, and you can paint a picture better than anyone I know. But tell me. What did you say? What did she say? I need details, man."

"I told her everything that you said, and she said she can be there Christmas Eve."

She let out a scream of joy. "Yes! Oh, Oliver. This is amazing. If you were here I'd kiss you on that smirking cheek. You're smirking, aren't you?"

"You know me."

"I don't even care. I'm glad you're just that good. This is awesome. I have to go and run and tell the gang."

"And Kevin," he said with an accusatory tone that sounded like it should be followed by "K-I-SS-ING."

"Yeah. Kevin. I can't wait to tell him too, but right now there's a group of people in the Chris Kringle Kitchen that are all going to be thrilled to hear that Polly's coming to town. I'll call you later. Thank you, Oliver. Thank you so much."

"All I did was answer the phone."

"Yeah, but you always do. Thanks for being the best friend ever." She disconnected the call and ran inside the diner.

Inside the Kringle Kitchen, Ezra was still

commiserating with his friends, while Carol freshened their hot chocolate.

As Lisa walked in Ezra ran a hand through his hair, trying to hold it together. "I appreciate how hard everyone tried to help, I really do, but it looks like we just don't have the resources to—"

She raced to the table, throwing her hands in the air. "I think I just got us one more chance at a buyer."

"What? How? Who?" Ezra's chair screeched across the tile floor as he leapt to his feet.

"Well, first of all. Slow down," she said to Ezra, trying to catch her breath. "Okay, my partner and I have this client named Polly, and Polly is looking to expand. So, we've convinced her to come to Evergreen during the Christmas Festival to look at the store."

Excitement rose, and everyone started talking at once. Ezra's face lit up. "That's amazing. It's great—"

"Let's not get ahead of ourselves," Lisa said. "We still have a lot of work to do to impress this woman. I just wish we…" she closed her eyes and looked up, wishing on nonexistent daytime stars for answers. "Oh boy." She tucked her hands into the back pockets of her jeans as she stood there thinking. She needed a miracle. Christmas magic. That's it! "The snow globe." Lisa locked eyes with Carol, then spun around. With everyone watching, she walked straight over to the front counter and lifted the snow globe off of its pedestal in its place of honor.

The wooden base felt smooth in her hands. It was

still as heavy as she remembered from her childhood. Her heart raced.

This snow globe was known to grant wishes. No one really knew how it came to be in the Kringle Kitchen. Some people said that it literally just showed up one day. Lisa eyed the replica of the Evergreen Church sitting upon the snowy hill with tall evergreen trees on each side. She yearned to be part of that happy couple who rode in a horse-drawn carriage in front of it...but right now, her wish was for the store.

She closed her eyes, gently turned the snow globe over, and gave it a good shake. The snow swirled around the church as she squeezed her eyes tight and made a wish. "Please work." She set snow globe back down and walked slowly back to the table, letting out the breath she'd been holding.

"What did you wish for?" David asked.

"Hold on a minute." Thomas raised his hand. "I thought we weren't supposed to tell our wishes."

"That's what people always say," Joe said.

Carol laughed. "Usually just before they tell us what they wished for." Carol turned to Lisa. "So, spill it."

"I wished for a new idea. And by the way, why don't people ever tell their wishes?" Lisa dropped her hands to her side. "I think that's kind of silly. If it's an important Christmas wish to you, I think you should just share it with people."

Michelle seemed to agree. "That's actually a good point."

David said, "That *is* why we write to Santa."

Lisa looked over at David. *Oh, to be a kid again.* "Yeah. It's... Wait a minute. What?" An idea niggled at her brain. She pointed to David. "Say that again."

"We tell Santa what we want? It's why we write him letters?" David looked completely confused.

"That's why we write him letters." Lisa took the old letter out of her pocket and tapped it against her other hand. "That's it. Kevin's letter." She tightened up, shaking the letter in the air. "That's it!"

Not one of them—not Thomas, Michelle, Joe, Carol, David, Hannah, or Ezra—seemed to know what the heck she was trying to say.

"The letter is the key. We use this letter to sell the store."

Hannah still looked dumbfounded. "Man. That snow globe works fast."

Michelle tilted her head. "So, like the candlelight processional?"

"Yes! All of it. The candlelight processional. The carols. The bells." Lisa's hands were flailing around with each exciting word. "All of it. Everything that is in this letter, we use it. 'Christmas like it used to be.'"

Ezra patted Hannah on the shoulder, nodding with interest. "It could work."

Michelle shook her head. "That's not going to be easy to pull off. Daisy kept some of the things going, but nobody did this like Ruth. And they did it with a lot more time to plan."

"I know." Lisa still held the letter between her

hands. She was so excited that tears blurred her vision a bit. "I know that. But I still think we have to try. And we can show Polly what Evergreen is really made of."

Lisa faced her new friends and held her hands out, face up. Closing her eyes, she said, "Please tell me you're with me."

It barely took a split second for all of them to raise their hands and shout in agreement. Everyone around the room seemed excited by the show of togetherness. A community pulling together. This was exactly why she loved small towns.

She raised her knee and both hands in the air. "Yes!"

The only person missing was Kevin. She wished she'd told him about the letter sooner. If she had, he'd have been here for this right now. She couldn't imagine how it felt to have something so personal from the past brought up so publicly after this much time. She had her own struggles with her childhood disappointments, and they weren't nearly as troubling as losing a parent.

Hopefully, he'd forgive her. And hopefully, he'd be excited that they might have a second chance to try to sell the place for Ezra and keep Daisy's Country Store, or something very similar, alive in Evergreen.

The next morning, low fog hung over the town. Lisa headed to Daisy's to take stock of what was done and what she had time to complete based on the new plan. She also needed to find Kevin and talk to him. And apologize again about the letter, too.

As she turned the corner into town square, she saw the familiar red truck parked in front of the store. Her hands tightened around her steering wheel.

She wasn't sure what she was going to say to him. As she pulled in front of the Kringle Kitchen, and got out of her car, she rehearsed possible speeches. She looked both ways, then crossed the street toward Daisy's.

To her surprise, Kevin was waiting outside with two coffee cups.

"Hey," he said with that smile that made the sides of his eyes crinkle slightly.

The way that made her insides spin.

"Hey." She made her way across the street.

Kevin lifted the cup in his left hand toward her. "Peppermint hot cocoa?"

Exactly how I like it. "Wow. You remembered."

"Yeah." He took her hand as she stepped over the mound of snow next to the sidewalk.

Her heart stammered as she took the cup from him. "Thank you. That's very sweet of you."

"I'm a very sweet guy."

They took a seat on the red bench in front of the store. She crossed her legs and tried to settle down. It wasn't going to be easy. So she dove right in.

"Listen, I just want to—"

"No, really, about yesterday. I'm sorry," he said. "I left really abruptly."

"No." Lisa shook her head. "It's not your fault."

"I heard about your plan. Use the old traditions to sell the store."

"Yeah?" Small towns were amazing like that. She was glad she wasn't trying to keep a secret.

"Evergreen has a newspaper, but most of us get our news at the coffee cart in the morning."

"Good, because I thought maybe you were a mind reader there for a second," Lisa teased.

But Kevin looked serious. "I want to help," he said.

"You do?"

"Yes. That's how Christmas is supposed to be in Evergreen."

Her heart filled with a warmth she'd never felt before. "Thank you."

He lifted his cup. "Cheers?"

"Cheers." She tapped her cup to his and took a sip.

Carol's voice carried across the street. "There they are." Carol crossed the square with Hannah awkwardly carrying Santa's mailbox. "Hannah had an idea about the Letters to Santa mailbox." Carol turned to Hannah. "Go."

Hannah stepped up, excited. "We'll continue the tradition and we'll set it up right here on Main Street."

"That's brilliant," Kevin said. Lisa liked the idea too, because the whole town would get to enjoy the old tradition now.

"And then once the store is up and running, we'll put it back in the store."

"I love it," Lisa said. "That's a great idea. And what about the choir and the caroling?"

"Don't you worry about that," Hannah assured her. "That's my baby. We're going to go set this up." Hannah and Carol headed down the street.

"This is great," Lisa said to Kevin. "I guess we should head on inside."

He stopped her. "But first. There's one more thing." He stood and reached for her hand to help her up.

"Ohhh. What's this? Mysterious."

"You're going to like this. Come on." He took her hand and they walked down the block to the Evergreen Church. He held the door for her as they stepped inside.

"Thank you, sir."

He led the way down to the basement.

What in the world does he want to show me down here? But when she reached the bottom step, she saw Henry standing near the bell mechanism with his toolbox at his side.

"Henry?" She walked over to Henry's side below the bell tower. Looking up, she could see the bottom of four stationary bells, plus the three above those that were visible from outside. Seven in all.

"I told Dad what you're trying to do. He agreed to come down and look at the bells again."

He was right. She did like this. "Oh, Henry. Thank you so much." She stepped closer, eyeing the complex set of gears that made up the clock and bell mechanisms.

Henry looked skeptical as he slipped on his glasses and looked closer at the green triangular mechanism. "Yeah. I'll take a look, Kev. I've worked on these bells for years, and I don't think we have all the parts." He snatched his glasses back off.

Both of the Miller men were clearly invested in these bells. She looked up in the tower, where a light dusting of snow coated the top of the bells. If only she had some advice. She thought again about the phrasing of the letter.

"Yeah, but the letter said—"

Kevin grabbed her hand and shushed her.

"What was that?" Henry asked.

"Oh, um, nothing," Lisa shrugged. She had no idea why Kevin didn't want his dad to know about the letter, but that was his call. "I just...do the best you can, Henry."

"If it doesn't work, it doesn't work." Kevin slapped his dad on his back.

Lisa smiled at Kevin. He looked happy.

Henry looked at the bells again, not appearing overly confident. As they walked off, she turned around to see Henry smiling at his son.

She bounded out of the basement, buoyed at the possibility of the bells finally chiming again. With Kevin right behind her they went back over to Daisy's.

"Thank you for asking your dad to look at the bells again."

"Couldn't hurt to try," he said. "It would be so great if after all these years we could get them working again. I wish you remembered what it was like. It was so…I guess magical is the best way to describe it. The loud, clear sounds of those bells. All seven carry a slightly different tone. It's musical. Heavenly."

A slight chill ran up her arms. She didn't remember the bells, but she hoped she'd get the chance to experience it herself this year.

Chapter Twelve

Michelle walked out of the Kringle Kitchen and then held the door for Thomas and David as they carried Santa's mailbox out to its new home on the square.

Carol might have been up to her matchmaking ways again—or stirring the pot, as Joe liked to say—but this time, Michelle didn't mind one bit. Carol had coerced Thomas into helping her by practically shoving the screw gun into his hand, and then she'd urged both of them, along with David, out the door.

"Thank you so much for helping out with this," Michelle said to Thomas.

Her comment seemed to amuse him. "Well, there's nowhere else we'd rather be."

David nodded as he helped carry the red mailbox over to the peppermint-striped pole that had been set up to support it. "It's cool that we can leave our letters to Santa right here."

"I used to leave my letters to Santa in this mailbox when I was your age. Everyone in town did."

Thomas turned and winked. Sometimes he almost seemed to be flirting. Like now. He smiled at her and sparks began to fly. She sucked in a breath. *Is he feeling this, too?*

The three of them made their way over to the post. It was awkward getting the mailbox up onto the pole, but finally it fell onto the notch and down into place. Thomas took the screws out of his pocket and began securing it.

"Would you look at this? Daisy's old mailbox." The joyful voice startled Michelle, and she turned around to see Nick. The old white-bearded man, wearing a blue pea coat and bright red scarf, seemed to have come out of nowhere.

"Hi, Nick." Michelle had hired him to play Santa last year, and he'd done such a great job she'd hired him on the spot for this year's festival before someone else could snatch him up.

David and Michelle held the mailbox steady as Thomas put another screw in the other side of the mounting bracket.

Michelle said to Nick, "You know Thomas and—"

"Of course I know David," Nick said. "He and Hannah came by the store the other day while I was there. How's the search for the lock coming?"

David hung his head. "Not great. We've tried just about everywhere."

"Well keep trying," Nick said with a glint in his

eye. "Sometimes the best way to solve a puzzle is to step back and wait. And then, a bell goes off in your head and everything makes sense."

David nodded. "Yeah. That makes sense." Thomas placed a reassuring arm around David's shoulder.

Nick addressed Thomas. "Are you new to Evergreen?"

"Trying to be," Thomas said. "In fact, we're thinking about branching out my logging business, setting up an office here in Evergreen."

What? She turned to him. "Really?"

"He's been talking about it for a whole day now," David said, rolling his eyes.

Michelle lit up inside like a Christmas tree. *This changes things.* Her heart raced.

"Wonderful," Nick said. "Keep up the good work. Putting the mailbox here is a wonderful idea."

Michelle held up the hand painted sign she'd painted for him to see. On a pine green painted board she'd painted, "Drop Your Letters (Or Thank-You Cards) To Santa Here."

Nick's snow-white beard wiggled as he spoke. "I'm sure Santa will appreciate that." He spun on his heel to leave.

"Bye, Nick." She held the sign by the red ribbon attached to the back. "Okay. Here we go." She hung it over the base, and it fit perfectly.

"Huh." Thomas stepped back, looking confused as he read it. "Thank-you cards?"

It made perfect sense to her. Of course, she was the

one who'd written it. "Everyone deserves a thank-you card, especially Santa."

David and Thomas both nodded. "You're right," David said.

"It's a little crooked," Thomas pointed out.

"Oh." She reached for the ribbon to adjust it. "I'll get it."

His hand got there first. Her hand closed on top of his. Together they shifted the ribbon to straighten the sign.

They both stepped away and Thomas looked down into Michelle's eyes. "Perfect."

Her gaze held his until she lowered her eyes. Yes, it seemed perfect.

He wrapped his arm around David, then took her hand.

She took a deep breath and went along for the moment. And a sweet moment it was.

Lisa was happy with the progress they were making on Daisy's, but she'd finished putting every trinket and decoration out and around the store, and it wasn't enough. The place looked empty. Uninteresting. Sure, there were little pockets that had risen to the challenge, but as a whole, it was disappointing. She'd been on the phone for the last twenty minutes trying to borrow some merchandise to fill the vast space, but she was running out of contacts.

Kevin stood and backed away from the counter

with a paint tray and brush in his hand. "Okay. Pipes are all done, and now this is done. Just have to let it dry." He spun around toward Lisa, then realized she was still on the phone. "Sorry," he mouthed.

She held up a finger. He stood there waiting, just smiling at her.

The repair on the counter was the last fix-it to-do on their list. The bones of the place were in good shape now, and it was amazing what some paint and wainscoting could do to brighten things up.

Lisa had her phone cradled to her shoulder. "No. That's okay. No. I appreciate it. Thank you, Shaun. Bye." She hung up and sighed.

Kevin set the paint aside. "Everything okay?"

"It will be as soon as I find somebody to give us some supplies." She tucked her phone in her back pocket. "Here's the thing. I need things that would go in a store, like pillows." She gestured to the empty shelves behind him. "And little Santa Claus people, and pretty stockings, and…what are you laughing at?"

"You," he said, amused. "You really love this."

"Yes. I do really love this. You know what I really love about it?" A blush rose in her cheeks. "I love that you can take something that no one else sees the potential in and you can turn it into something beautiful like we're doing with this store."

He shook his head. "It's amazing." He took a second and stood there just smiling at her. "I always see my job through this lens of what's not done yet. I always feel like I'm behind, and am completely focused on getting it done, but you…you enjoy the process. It's… it's so refreshing." He picked up his jacket. "Watching someone get so excited makes me realize that I've been ignoring the fact that that's the most interesting part. The potential."

Exactly. What were his thoughts were on their potential? Did he get those feelings when they touched like she did? She pondered Oliver's advice. Kevin had his jacket on, and technically he was done with what he'd committed to. It was kind of now or never.

"Hey." Lisa's heart beat a little faster, and she fidgeted with her phone.

He stopped and looked her way.

"I've got to run over to the inn and pick up a few things," she said. "Why don't you take a break and ride with me? And we'll get some dinner."

"Oh." He looked a little torn. "I have a thing I have to do."

Momentarily rebuffed, she regretted letting herself think there might be something more. What was I thinking? "Oh, never—"

"No. Look, I'm late as it is, but rain check?"

She settled back, disappointed. "You should go."

He was practically running for the door. *What in the world?* She felt like she was dumped…but that was totally stupid, because she'd already said she didn't even know if he liked her.

Oliver was wrong. Kevin didn't like her either way.

"Rain check? Good. Okay," he said as he closed the door behind him.

"Fine."

But it wasn't fine. She stood there bewildered. And confused. Had she really misread his signals?

And on top of the personal pity party, she still didn't have a resolution for the store. She hoped she hadn't just made things so awkward with Kevin that he wouldn't want to help her finish the job. She had to up the game if Polly was going to fall in love with this place. There wasn't much else she could do until she found a way to fill the shelves, so there was no reason for her to stick around, either.

With her coat over her shoulder she jogged to her car and drove back over to the inn. Lights from the Christmas trees inside glowed through the windows of the house. Each window had its own single bulb candle, too. A beautiful and simple look, but even that didn't improve her mood.

Lisa parked her car and walked up to the inn. When she stepped inside, the aroma of ham and the sweet and savory spices of holiday foods whetted her appetite.

A string trio played classic Christmas songs in front of the living room fireplace as guests in dress clothes dined. From here Lisa saw the table of desserts, including one of those fancy Buche de Noel cakes: a chocolate log. She'd never tasted one, but she'd always thought they looked so pretty.

Megan carried an hors d'oeuvre tray of cherry tomatoes and mozzarella balls shaped into a wreath atop a bed of basil into the dining room. "Are you having fun?" she asked the crowd.

The guests raised their glasses of wine and murmured their satisfaction.

She set down the tray, then spread her arms open. "Enjoy!" On her way back to the kitchen she bumped into Lisa in the foyer. "Hey."

"Hey," said Lisa.

"You're just in time. Dinner's ready."

"Great." Only she didn't really feel like eating at all now.

"Come with me for a sec." Megan took Lisa by the arm. "Let's put up some decorations."

"Okay." Lisa never turned down the chance to play Christmas. She followed Megan into the den.

"Aww. It's pretty." Megan had started decorating the tree that Kevin had brought over. Fresh cranberry garland was pretty against the little gold lights. There were only a few decorations up so far, but they were all the blown glass ornaments she'd made. Absolutely dazzling. She turned to Megan.

"You're doing this all alone?"

"Yeah," she said with a shrug.

Lisa placed her coat on the chair near the door. "Megan, everybody loves decorating a tree. I'm sure any one of those guests in there would love to help you."

"Which reminds me. I should check on the new guest. He just arrived from Boston…"

"Oh. Okay." Lisa picked up a couple of ornaments

and carried them over to the tree to hang them. Anything was better than sulking about Kevin.

A familiar voice came from the other room. "And he figured he could use a little R&R while helping out a friend."

Lisa froze and then squealed at the sound of Oliver's voice. She turned around. There he was, looking dapper as usual, in a blue sweater that matched his blue eyes. She ran and threw her arms around him in a big hug, one ornament still hanging from each of her hands. "Oliver! What are you doing here?" Megan stood there with her mouth wide.

"What's Christmas without my bestie?"

"Aww. Megan, this is Oliver."

"Oh, we've met. But he didn't tell me he knew you."

"I live for surprises," Oliver said.

"I know you do." Lisa couldn't believe her luck. Oliver's familiar presence was exactly what she needed right now while she was feeling so low about Daisy's and Kevin. Her mood quickly rebounded. "I'm so glad you're here."

"Excuse me a second," Megan said. "Someone is waving me down from the other room."

As Megan left, Lisa turned to Oliver. "You're the best thing that's happened to me all day. Here." She handed him one of the ornaments. "Help me decorate."

"Sure." As always, he fit right in to any situation. They walked over to the tree together.

"There you go." He stepped back, admiring the

ornament he'd just hung on a branch near the top, and then reached for another.

"You got here fast." Lisa hung her ornament on the other side of the tree.

"There's a shockingly adorable train that runs right into Evergreen."

"Yeah. I know the one." She poked her head around the tree. "I just didn't know you knew about it."

"I'm very resourceful." He gave her a wink. "In fact, I happened to have already been on it when I talked to you. Plus, you said you needed the help."

He'd been on his way before she'd even asked. Like finishing her sentences, he was always right there when she needed him. "Oliver, I do need your help. The shelves are completely bare. The decorations look amazing. You know me. I can stage a store with no merchandise at all, but this is Polly we're talking about here. She's going to expect—"

Oliver held an ornament between his fingers. "Wow, this is gorgeous," he interrupted her mid-sentence.

"Yeah. They are. Aren't they? Polly's gonna expect stuff like that. Handmade and…" Her eyes narrowed. Those ornaments were just the thing. The answer had been right in front of her all along. "You know what you are?" She danced around a bit. "You're brilliant, Oliver." She barely contained her excitement. "I have an idea. Come with me." She pulled him by the arm toward the door.

"Let me grab my coat." Oliver ran back and grabbed his coat from the coat rack in the hall.

They put on their coats as they dashed to her car.

"Where are you taking me?" Oliver slid into the passenger seat.

"This is so perfect!" She drummed the steering wheel and gunned the engine, her tires spinning before catching traction in the snow.

A few minutes later they were in the town square parked across from the church. The sounds of "Joy to the World" filled the air as they got out of the car. The music transfixed Lisa, distracting her from her mission.

She grabbed Oliver by the hand and crossed the street to the church. "The music is coming from in here." She opened the fairy-tale tall door, then poked her head inside.

Thomas and David sat in the third pew on the left. Fourteen people all dressed in deep burgundy choir robes lined the front of the altar. With the beautiful stained-glass window behind them and all the greenery and lights they looked like a band of angels, and their sound was heavenly.

Hannah conducted them in animated fashion, her body almost acting as another instrument guiding the glorious sound. Among those singing were Michelle, Carol, Henry, and then Lisa saw Kevin. *This is what he had to do? The thing?*

She and Oliver slipped into one of the smooth wooden pews in the back of the small church. There were only two rows of eight pews here. The sound of those perfectly blended voices rose beautifully around her, sending a zing of comfort and joy through her.

She was dying to tell Oliver about Kevin turning her down for dinner because he had a thing. For this, as it turned out. She hadn't been able to take her eyes off of Kevin since she walked in. She wondered if Oliver had noticed.

Oliver leaned in, a bemused expression on his face. "So your idea...is choir practice?"

"Not exactly, but..." Lisa watched them singing. Kevin looked right at her and smiled. Her heart skipped.

The choir brought the carol to a finish. Lisa and Oliver clapped wildly.

"Great job." Hannah applauded them, too. "Let's take five, okay?" As the choir members came down, Hannah said to one of the members, "That was so good. Thank you."

Lisa hung back as Thomas and David went to the front to catch up with Michelle. Kevin came down the aisle, never taking his eyes off of her.

She stood up and stepped out of the pew, clearing her throat. "Hi," she said.

"Hi."

"Choir practice?"

"Yeah. I sang in high school." He blushed a little as he took off the choir robe, revealing a long sleeved black T-shirt.

"So, choir practice is the thing that you had to do."

She couldn't stop smiling. She'd been so disappointed when he turned her down.

"I wanted to have dinner with you." He shook his head. "I really did, but I promised."

"You are full of surprises, Mr. Miller." *Good ones.*

"I know. It's ridiculous. I should have just said what it was, but it sounded like a terrible excuse."

"No. It's handsome." *Did I just say that out loud?* "It's cute," she tried badly to recover. "No. I mean…"

Oliver sprung from his seat and put his arm around Lisa. "Hi, I'm Oliver. I work with Lisa in Boston and all over."

Thanks for the save, Oliver. "Yes. You do," she said, still totally embarrassed. "And this is—" she pointed to Kevin.

"Kevin." Kevin filled in the blank, then shook Oliver's hand. "I work with Lisa. Here. Now."

"Yes. Now. Here," Lisa repeated, stepping away from Oliver and closer to Kevin. She was jabbering. Ever since Oliver called her out on the crush on Kevin, it had her all tripped up.

The guys just sort of nodded at each other. For a split second, in a weird sort of way, it almost seemed like a standoff.

It had to be her imagination. She pushed the silly notion aside as Hannah and Carol walked toward her.

"Hey, come here," Lisa called out to them. "I had an idea. Do you remember the other day when we were downstairs in the basement? There were those boxes with all the arts and crafts for the Christmas Festival. You showed me your hats?"

"Oh yeah," said Hannah. "And now that we moved everything to town square, we're barely finding space for all the stuff that goes in all the booths."

This worked to her favor. "Okay," Lisa said. "What if we put all that inventory in storage in Daisy's store?"

Oliver knew exactly what she meant. He turned to Hannah and Carol. "It would give it the appearance of an actual store with merchandise and customers."

"Yes. We can feature the local artisans." Lisa looked for a response.

"It's great," Kevin said.

"I love it," Carol and Hannah echoed.

Carol was excited. "We have quilters. We have ornament makers. We even have a maple syrup sugar shack in town."

"Mmm." Lisa could almost taste it.

"Well, someone show me these boxes," Oliver said.

"You got it." Carol took Oliver by the hands and led him downstairs. "Come on."

"It's awesome. Great idea." Hannah excused herself to meet with the other choir members still lingering in the church.

Lisa turned and started walking toward the door to the basement with Kevin right behind her. "So, I guess we should just—"

"No. I should head back to the store." Kevin walked right out the front door.

"Oh? Oh yeah." She closed the door. "Then, I'll..."

She followed him outside, thinking she'd go over with him.

"Yeah. I'll see you later." His smile seemed forced as he turned and walked away in the snow.

"Okay." *What just happened here?*

Chapter Thirteen

Michelle and Thomas walked out of the church right behind David and Hannah after choir practice. Thomas's hand grazed Michelle's and stole her breath. Her knees wobbled as if they were made of gelatin. *So this is what getting swept off of your feet is like.*

The snow fell around them and the air held an icy nip to it. A splendid winter evening.

Just ahead, Nick crossed their path, and stopped in front of David and Hannah. "How's that key search going?"

"We've tried everywhere." David held the key in the air. The poor kid hadn't set that key down except to eat for the last few days.

"He's right." Hannah shrugged. "I'm starting to think that key doesn't go to anything in Evergreen."

Nick looked shocked. "Don't lose heart." He glanced up at the church tower for more than a fleeting glance. "I'm sure you're closer than you think." Nick turned and went on his jolly way with a little jig in his jog.

David looked like he was tiring of the mystery. "Maybe we can try again after ice skating."

"Sure we can." Hannah hugged him closer to her. "Let's go have some fun. Will we see you over there, Michelle?"

"I'm on hot cocoa duty," Michelle said. "Of course you will."

"Great." Hannah and David took off toward the ice skating rink.

"I'll catch up," Thomas called after Hannah.

She turned around with a broad smile and gave him a thumbs up. "No hurry."

Michelle watched David take Hannah's hand and run toward the old wooden bridge. She swallowed and took a deep breath.

"Thank you for coming to hear the choir. We're better in performance than we are in rehearsal." Michelle's nerves seemed to vibrate. She didn't even really know what to talk about, but she loved that he'd shown up and it hadn't taken long for her to realize he wasn't there to just be a supportive brother to Hannah. With him watching, she'd almost forgotten the words to "The First Noel." Not that she was complaining.

He took her hand. "You were very good in rehearsal. I really enjoyed listening."

Her hand in his only made talking that much harder. "It's always good to have an audience. It changes it up. You hear it differently. So, anytime you want to come listen—"

Abruptly, Michelle quit babbling. She reached up and kissed him softly on the lips. Just a peck, but she'd done it.

She touched her lips. *Why did I just do that? I should apologize.* But nothing came out of her mouth.

He looked surprised, but he didn't look unhappy. Maybe if she could say something. Anything. He would just forget it.

Thomas leaned forward and returned the kiss, but he didn't just give her a little peck.

He kissed her like she'd always wanted to be kissed.

She pulled away. Yes, she'd started this, but maybe she shouldn't have. She'd just met him. He didn't even live in this town, and he might have said he was considering opening up a branch of his business here, but that wasn't a done deal, either. And there was David. Although he was such a great kid, that made things more complicated.

"So. That," Michelle pointed to his lips and smiled.

"Exactly. That."

They both laughed, and that calmed her down. She finally gathered the strength to just open up. "Is it… is this fast?" Michelle wrapped her arm around his. "Does it feel fast to you?"

"It feels nice to me, but we can go at whatever pace you'd like. I'm in no hurry. I'm really liking getting to know you."

Michelle smiled at him. *He's such a good man.* She'd never complain about Carol's matchmaking again.

"I really like getting to know you too. You and David." She sank into his shoulder, still clinging to his arm as they walked over the old wooden bridge to the skating rink.

The bridge shone under the holiday lights, and the skaters below looked like they belonged in a miniature Christmas village. She could picture the three of them spending time together there one day.

Lisa and Oliver had spent the last two hours moving boxes of arts and crafts from the basement of the church to the first floor, and then used the handcart to truck them around the corner to Daisy's. She had more than enough to fill Daisy's Country Store with merchandise now, and the items were beautiful and colorful and handcrafted. It was going to look amazing.

Lisa walked over to the shelves near the front window of the store. "I'm thinking we can use this area over here for the pillows, and then the maple syrup over there, or wait…maybe we do all the food-related items up on the second level." She held a finger to her lips.

"I like that. All food stuffs together. Plus the old Hoosier cabinet lends itself to kitchen-related goods." Oliver moved a couple of boxes. "Here it is. There's a whole box of embroidered flour sack towels. These could really soften up the display of the recipes in a jar and the maple syrup."

"Nice. It's all coming together. I'm so glad you're here to help." She raised her hands in the air. "We've got this, Daisy. Polly is going to be wowed."

"I think you're right. These arts and crafts are a notch above what you'd expect at a festival. This is great," Oliver agreed.

They made decisions on where each box of things would go. Moving the boxes in front of the cases and then marking them with what shelves or details so that other people could help them unload the boxes and fill the spaces.

"I'm exhausted," Lisa admitted. "Let's go back to the inn and take a little break. After dinner we can come back and get a few things done and then really get down to business tomorrow."

"Sure thing."

She tossed her keys to him. "You drive."

They zipped around the corner and went inside. Megan greeted them with a hello. "Good to see you two. I have mulled wine in the kitchen. Help yourselves."

Lisa closed her eyes, then opened them and looked to Oliver. "See why I love this place?"

"Mulled wine for two," Oliver said as he headed to the kitchen.

"Just half a cup for me," Lisa said. "Then we need to go grab some dinner at the Kringle Kitchen and get back to work." Lisa sat down on the loveseat near the front window, looking at the Christmas tree they'd been working on. Megan had finished it and it looked beautiful. Lisa kicked off her boots and put her aching feet, in red and white striped socks, up on the coffee table.

Oliver came back into the room with two Christmas mugs. "I get the feeling you almost don't want to leave Evergreen. What changed?"

"Well, it's not just this town. It's the people." Could she even explain it? "It sounds crazy. But it feels like magic to me." Not magic, but magical. Her heart was at peace here. "It feels like home." The fire snapped and crackled beside them. "And then there's—"

"Kevin." Oliver completed her sentence.

"Am I that obvious?"

He gave a hearty laugh. "Just a little."

She couldn't deny it. "I mean, he's smart. He's driven, and he's super talented. He makes me laugh." She looked over to Oliver. "On more than one occasion, too."

"Well, you do love that."

"Yeah, I do love that." Even just talking about Kevin warmed Lisa's heart.

Lisa looked into the fire. She'd really given this some thought and it was now coming out like it always did when she was with Oliver. He was truly her best friend. She was so thankful for him.

"It'd be different if I was going to be in one place for more than a while, but—"

"You're still holding onto that grab-a-bag-and-go thing, huh?" Oliver said.

"I'm just not sure I want to stop traveling," Lisa said, but she wasn't sure what she wanted to do, either. She loved her job, and traveling for it had always been so enjoyable. But being here. In Evergreen. It had been so much. In so many ways. She liked the way it felt.

"We have some time, but I'd really like to open a store with you in Boston," Oliver said. "And we have a good amount of savings, but Boston is definitely more expensive than other places. I'm wondering if it's really that you love the traveling, or that you're starting to change your mind about Boston being the place you'll eventually put down roots."

She hadn't really considered that, but now that he'd laid it out there, he had a good point. But that was the good thing about their friendship. They could say or do anything and know that there'd be no judgment or hurt feelings.

"Oliver, I'm glad you said that. I hadn't realized it, but maybe this has been in the back of my mind, or my heart, all along."

"You know I don't believe in coincidences. I think everything happens for a reason."

She nodded.

"And when I said I thought you'd be wearing an elves' costume and helping Santa, I was only half-joking."

"I haven't signed up to do that yet, but making this store a focal point of the Christmas holiday is a good second to that."

Chapter Fourteen

Outside, Kevin walked up to the inn. He owed her an apology for running off again. He didn't know what came over him. Well, yes he did. The whole Oliver thing. It got under his skin, but he'd jumped to conclusions more than once with her already. He should just ask her about it.

As he got closer, he saw the back of Lisa's head. His mood lifted…and then he saw Oliver sitting awfully close to her on that loveseat by the fire where the stockings were hung. Like a couple. Fine, it was an inn and those were not their stockings, but something about the image gave him pause. Was his gut right? Was there more to Oliver and Lisa than business partners?

There was only one way to find out. He'd ask.

Mustering courage, he opened the front door, and began to step inside. He heard them talking. About Boston. About their savings. About them opening a store together, and about her wanting to still travel.

There was no room for him in her plan.

I've been fooling myself. She needed a contractor, and I fulfilled that need. Now she'll be moving on.

He slowly closed the door and left, feeling more alone than he'd ever felt before. Turning his back on her was the hardest thing he'd ever done, but he had to. He walked back to the truck, barely noticing how frigid the temperatures were tonight. The lanterns along the path back to his truck seemed to mock him as he walked by. How had he been so stupid?

He went back to the store to finish up the work he'd agreed to do. The sooner he got done and made good on his promise to Lisa, the sooner he could leave the town in his rearview mirror.

At Daisy's, he attacked the last of the list with a vengeance. A few minor repairs, replacing knobs and tightening things up, gave him too much headspace to think. He fired up the floor sander and let the noise of the machine drown out his thoughts about Lisa.

It didn't take long. He wasn't going for pristine flooring, but rather just cleaning up the charm of the original one. He swept, vacuumed, and then caught any other dust particles with a cloth dampened with mineral spirits. The finish was the key in these projects. He set up the fans and heaters to help things dry quicker, then put a coat of white paint on the floors, working from the sides in, then down the center aisle out the door. Tomorrow, he'd come back and mark off and paint the black squares like they'd discussed.

The wet sheen made the whole store look new. Lisa had done a great job staging it so far, and she hadn't rushed through it like he'd worried she would. No job deserved a shortcut. He locked the door and hung the "wet floor" sign on the door handle to keep anyone from trekking across his hard work.

As he turned around, Lisa came walking out of the Kringle Kitchen with a smile. His heart stammered.

"Hey," she said. "I was just coming over to see if you—"

"I sanded and put the first coat of paint on the floor, needs to dry overnight, so until then there's nothing more to do." He focused on the gloves in his hand. Stacking and restacking them. Anything to avoid those beautiful eyes.

"Oh? Well, I thought we were going to do that later, and Oliver and I could've helped you."

The guy's name made Kevin's gut ache, even if she was alone right now. "No. Do your thing." He pasted a smile on his face. As much as his clenched jaw would allow. "How's Oliver settling in?"

"It's taking him a minute to get used to a small town, but he's okay. He's good. An extra pair of hands never hurts."

I could do without them. The thought was cut short when Oliver came out of the Kringle Kitchen, holding a cup of coffee. Kevin felt his jaw twitch.

"Hey." Oliver bounded into the middle of their conversation. "Do they call it the Kringle Kitchen all year round?" Oliver said, making a joke out of it. "Or do they change that during the summer?"

"They put little shorts on the Santa Claus on the

sign in summer," Kevin said. "It's a bit of a wedding destination."

"Tourist towns know what they're doing," Oliver said.

"Yeah." Kevin put his gloves on.

Lisa gave a small smile. "Kevin said that since we don't have access to the store, we should go to the ice-skating pond."

Kevin shook his head. "I don't remember saying anything about—"

"There's an ice-skating pond?" Oliver leaned in with excitement.

"I knew you would like that," Lisa said.

"Where is it?"

Kevin would be glad to be rid of him. "Just over the bridge." *Off you go.*

"What are we doing just standing here? Do they rent skates?"

Kevin nodded. "Yeah."

"Apparently, yes," she said. "Meet you there?"

"Oh?" Oliver looked a little confused, but he grabbed his hat and put it on his head. "Okay. See you there."

Oliver rushed off.

"See you guys," Kevin said, making a hasty exit.

Lisa caught his arm. "Why don't you come along?"

Kevin was torn. Why torture himself? She'd be leaving town soon, anyway.

She tossed her head toward the path. "Walk with me."

He should do what his mind was telling him, which was to beat feet out of there, but his heart was keeping him at her side. "Sure." His adrenaline danced through his veins. The cold snowy night could've been a summer afternoon and he wouldn't have noticed the difference.

They walked down the street and then over the footbridge, which was teeming in brilliant cool white lights. The skaters looked tiny below.

"This is where I learned to skate," he told her, thinking back to when his parents brought him down here. As a kid, Mom would walk him here. She'd watch him skate for hours, and never missed a hockey match, either. Those early skating lessons and hours of practice had paid off big time. He wished she could've seen it. And he wished she could've met Lisa. She would've liked Lisa. "It's a pretty special place." She was special, too.

"Yeah."

He stopped at the middle of the bridge, under the tallest point of the beams. "Here's a good view." He led her to the handrail.

"Aww." She took in a deep breath, bouncing with excitement as she leaned over the garland-draped railing with the snow falling around her. Small flakes landed in her hair and on her coat. "Oh gosh. It's gorgeous."

A couple dozen people skated the shiny ice, some better than others. Bundled against the chilly temperatures, everyone was bundled from head to toe.

The lights on the trees surrounding the frozen rink reflected, giving the view a heavenly glow. He turned to watch Lisa enjoying the scene.

She caught him watching her. "What?"

"It's just the way you look at this town," Kevin said. "You see the best of it. It's nice."

"Well, Hannah told me people have been skating on this pond for over a hundred years. So, what's not to love about that, right?"

Love. He put his elbows on the railing, standing so close to her he caught the flowery smell of her shampoo.

Oliver's voice broke the mood. "Come on down. The ice is warm." He sped around the ice, clapping his hands and laughing so loudly Kevin heard it all the way up on the bridge. Oliver went swooshing by, then swept wide and pulled into a tight spin, with a fancy twist.

"Oh, yeah. Bronze medal," Lisa explained.

Figures. An athlete too. "Seems like you two have got it all figured out, huh?"

"We do share a brain," she joked. "It's kind of like when you spend that much time with someone, you become a pretty solid team."

"Must be nice." Kevin watched Oliver below. "Every job I take, I get this whole new crew of guys. Takes work to catch them up and get them on board with my way of doing things."

"Yeah, and you have to find a new place to get supplies."

"Plus, living out of a suitcase," he said.

"Yep."

"And laundromats, and staying single the whole time."

Lisa nodded in agreement. "You know, Oliver and I are both always complaining about being single."

Kevin brows furrowed. "Wait. What?"

"What?"

"You and Oliver aren't…" He had to have heard her wrong.

She blinked. "We're?"

"…a thing?"

Lisa's face twisted. "No." Then she busted out laughing. "No."

"I guess I just thought—"

"No. We're not a thing. We met in college. We went on one date, but both instantly knew it was not a thing. We've been best friends since."

Relief whooshed through him, and when he looked back down at the rink, Oliver wasn't his focus, but rather the kids and the couples. Oliver pushed a young boy in a skate trainer. A good sport.

Lisa leaned back. "Look. Oliver and I are best friends, but that's where it ends."

His mouth snapped shut, but inside, he was doing a happy dance over the news. In his defense they'd looked pretty cozy together at the inn. Her bright eyes still held his gaze. He swallowed past the knot that just formed in his throat. "Well, I guess instead of jumping to conclusions I should've—"

"Gotten the whole story?" She raised an eyebrow.

"Yeah. Embarrassing." But the good news lifted the shadows in his heart.

"It is," she said. "It is embarrassing. For one of us." Her tone was cocky, but the look in her eye was playful. "And that is why I'm going to save you right now, and ask you to skate." She let her hand drag across his back as she walked behind him leading the way to the rink.

"I'd love to," he said, turning to join her.

The pond was quartered off with pines lit up in alternating red, blue, and green with sparkly icy snow mounds around the edges to keep the skaters safely on the thickest ice.

The hot cocoa stand was set up at the left edge. Michelle stood with Hannah next to Joe. They were all bundled in their wool coats, warm scarves, and gloves, ready to help serve. Around the stand, Christmas trees decorated in red and gold balls stood on each side of a table covered in a red tablecloth with candles and brightly decorated Christmas packages in the front. Joe arranged hot chocolates on a tray for the chilly ice skaters.

"Looking good, David," Joe called as David sped by with Thomas coming up quickly behind him. Thomas threw his arm up in the air and gave Joe a thumbs up.

Hannah leaned in to Michelle. "I'm really glad you and my brother seem to be getting closer."

"Yeah. We are. And you're sure?" Michelle lowered her eyes. "I mean it's not weird or anything for you?"

"Why would it be weird? I've never seen you this happy," Hannah said. "Either of you, in fact."

Michelle sighed. "I wanted to talk to you about it, but I didn't want to stir up hurt feelings either. With you and Charlie breaking up, it just seemed like bad timing."

Hannah put her hands up. "Hey. There are no hard feelings between Charlie and me. I'm grateful for the time we spent together. I'm grateful I got to know someone special who loves the holidays as much as I do. It made for a fun Christmas Festival last year, but it just wasn't enough to build a whole relationship on. We're both okay with that. We'll remain good friends." Hannah lips pursed. "I did learn a very valuable lesson though."

"What's that?"

"I learned you have to be very specific with those snow globe wishes. I got exactly what I asked for. A guy who loved Christmas as much as me, not the man I would spend the rest of my life with."

"Oh, Hannah." Michelle hugged her. "I'd really hoped he was the one."

"I think we both wanted that too. The right one will come along. I'm not worried. We just got swept away a little too fast to notice what was really going on."

Michelle's face dropped. "Swept away is exactly how I feel about Thomas."

"No. That doesn't mean people shouldn't get swept away, Michelle. It just means that sometimes you don't know how long something will last, but you do it anyway because it might." She took Michelle's hands. "Don't you let my experience scare you from a chance with my brother."

Joy rose inside Michelle.

Thomas and David skated up and came to a stop next in front of the hot cocoa table. "Whew. Hey guys," Thomas said.

"Michelle, come skate with us," David said, nearly breathless from the exertion.

"Yeah," Thomas said. "Come on."

Michelle looked up at Thomas, who smiled, then over to Hannah, who motioned for her to go for it.

"Oh, go ahead." Joe encouraged her too. "We've got the cocoa covered."

"Don't expect any fancy moves out of me," she warned them. "But I'm gonna do my best." She came around the table, a little wobbly on her skates.

"We've got you," Thomas promised.

"I'm not really good at this." She waved her arms as she lost balance, but David took her hand and Thomas skated up on the other side of her and off they went, laughing all the way.

Kevin caught Lisa's hand in his as they walked down to the shack to rent skates. Once they'd gotten them, they walked over to one of the bright red wooden benches around the edge of the pond. They sat close, lacing their skates.

"You ready for this?" His competitive nature was already wanting to race her.

"Probably not as ready as you are." She tightened her laces and stood, then they both glided toward the entrance of the rink. A white filmy tent formed a pretty tunnel of lights and the entrance to the ice rink.

They skated out onto the ice hand in hand, which just reassured him more that she and Oliver were just friends. Music piped in from all points around the rink like a concert.

He hadn't skated in a while, but he had muscle memory from all those years playing hockey, and she was steady on her feet. They skated like a practiced couple nearly half way around the rink, then he tugged on her hand and they spun around without so much as a wobble.

Oliver sped by, continuing to leap and jump and do spins that would probably still earn him a spot on the Olympic figure skating team.

Kevin placed the hand on the small of Lisa's back, holding her other hand tight in his own. When she looked up into his face, his heart warmed.

Thomas and Michelle skated by. Michelle slipped, and Thomas held onto her, keeping her from falling. Kevin gave him a nod.

"Let's get some hot cocoa," Kevin said, steering Lisa behind the stand.

"Sounds good. We can share one."

He liked the sound of that. Joe extended the tray toward them and Kevin took a white cup with red snowflakes on it, holding the straw out to Lisa first.

She took a sip. "So good. And warm."

"Are you too cold?"

She slowly lifted her eyes to his. "No. This is perfect."

His heart turned over as he looked into her eyes.

Chapter Fifteen

That night after Lisa and Oliver went back to the inn, Kevin was in such a good mood that he returned to the store and finished painting the floors. He wasn't usually a fan of painting old wood floors, but he had to admit it was a good remedy for the short haul. Besides, there was no way he was going to be able to sleep, so having this to work on was a gift.

He was happy with how it had turned out. He was sure she would be, too. Maybe they were cutting corners a little, but there would be time after the festival to put topcoats on and finish the job. He was starting to learn how to make compromises, and that wasn't a bad thing.

It would look perfect when Lisa got to the store in the morning, even though the last step wouldn't be complete. He couldn't wait for her to see it.

In the morning, he got there early and got coffee. He was standing there waiting on her when she showed up at nine. They only had a few minutes to enjoy their coffee before a steady stream of townsfolk started showing up, dropping off more things that they'd been storing for their booths.

They now had more than enough merchandise to use in the staging for Polly's visit in two days when she showed up for the Christmas Eve festival. People seemed excited to have their wares displayed before the festival even began.

Kevin stood at the back of the store watching Lisa greet people with true enthusiasm over their handiwork. Her positive spirit lifted his. For the first time, maybe ever, he looked around enjoying the accomplishment, not making a list of what was left to do. It was a bit freeing.

Lisa helped a woman set up her collection of soft sculpture snowmen on one row of shelving. Floor to ceiling, those jolly stuffed snowmen filled up the whole column. All different sizes and colors, each one brought a little more life to the store.

He directed people to different areas based on the layout Lisa had shared with him. That way, the boxes would be in the right general location for unloading. Oliver stood on a ladder moving some of the items they'd found in the back of Daisy's up to the top row to make room for the local artisans' more attractive items.

"Coming through," Hannah said, her arms full, as the bells rang on the door. David came dragging in behind her with two bags in each hand. "I have the rest of my hats here."

"Great!" Lisa jogged around the far counter where she'd begun setting up a Nativity, hand-carved by an elderly man on the outskirts of town. She ran over and helped Hannah set her box on the counter. "At least they're light."

"Yeah, I don't know what I was thinking, putting them in a box this big. It was awkward to carry."

David lifted his bags. "I tried to tell her to put them in bags. This was easy." He lifted them in the air.

"You're a good helper, David," Lisa complimented him. "I found something that I think might work pretty well for your hats. Come with me." Lisa and Hannah walked back to the storage room. A countertop spinning rack with a tall pole on top sat in the corner. "I thought we could use some of the bright wrapping paper and kind of wad it into a half circle and then tug the hats on top of that so they'd sit on each of these spindles. They'd look pretty and people could spin the display around to find the one they liked best."

"Perfect," Hannah said. "How do you think of this stuff?"

"I don't know. It's what I do," she said with a modest lift of her shoulder. "Plus these are great. I want to show them off." She grabbed one side of the display. "Help me carry it. We'll put it on the counter near the door. The bright colors will draw people's attention and pull them right into the store."

"You know all the tricks," Hannah said.

They carried the display out front and set it up. It didn't take long to get the hats all floofed and situated.

Where Hannah had multiples of the same style and color, they staggered them in the glass display case below. It looked like a high-end boutique arrangement.

"I've got pretty price cards, too." Hannah reached for a manila envelope in the bottom of the box. The tags were glossy white card stock. She'd whip-stitched yarn around the edge for a unique border with "Hats by Hannah" stamped in pretty script in the middle.

"Oh my gosh. These price tags are as awesome as the hats. Don't tell me you're one of those people that can make those cool cards with the cutouts and stamps and stuff."

Hannah rolled her eyes. "Guilty."

"I wish I could do that." Lisa shook her head. "I've never tried, but it looks so detailed. I'm not sure if I'm patient enough to sit that still."

"I'll show you sometime."

"I'd love that." Lisa placed the price tag tents in the case, then helped Hannah tuck the individual price tags into each hat.

Hannah pulled a soft pink cap onto her head. It had a wide band and a loose top, giving it kind of a French beret look. "This is a new pattern this year. What do you think?"

"I love it." Lisa sorted through the box, finally picking out a red one to try on. "How does mine look? Oui?"

"It looks great on you."

Lisa snapped her fingers. "We need a mirror here for when people are trying on the hats."

"You're right." Hannah squinted her eyes a little. "I might I have an old mirror in my garage. I'll check tonight."

"Perfect. If it's small, we can put it up on the counter. If it's tall, then we might be able to get Kevin to hang it over there for us. Either would work fine."

Kevin helped the maple syrup folks set up their display on the second level, next to displays of mason jar food gifts with everything from dried beans and organic pet treats to cookie mixes and soup ingredients. The store was filling up fast. When he finished with the maple syrup display, he walked across the street and ordered lunch to bring back for him and Lisa.

As he waited at the counter to place his to-go order, he overheard a couple of people talking about how excited they were that Daisy's might reopen. He was proud to be a part of that.

"What can I get for you, Kevin?" Carol asked.

"A couple ham and cheese sandwiches on whole wheat toast, lettuce, tomato, pickles, and your delicious house dressing, and two waters to go."

"Got it. Just give me a minute and I'll have it right up for you."

"Sounds good." He leaned against the counter, waiting and watching the activity in the store across the street. Lisa never stopped. One minute she was arranging merchandise, the next she was greeting someone coming into the store or saying goodbye. It was like she'd been a part of this community the whole time.

Carol swept around the counter with a bag. "That'll be ten dollars even." She leaned forward and winked. "Contractor discount."

"Thanks, Carol." He paid her and then walked back across the street. When Kevin opened the door to Daisy's, Hannah was getting ready to leave. He held the door for her, and Lisa caught it as she said goodbye to Hannah.

"Bye, Hannah." He held up the bag and motioned to Lisa. "I got lunch for us."

"I'm starving. Thank you." Lisa fell in step behind him as he led the way to the vintage porcelain top table and chairs they'd set up in the food section. It gave the place a real kitchen vibe. Especially now that the shelves were filled with all the colorful products.

He spread out the lunch like a picnic. She plopped down in one of the chairs and took one of the bottles of water.

"Thank you so much," she said. "For this. For everything."

"Don't mention it." He sat down in the chair next to her. "I'm really enjoying it."

"I'm glad." She looked a little tired, but happy.

"I hope you like ham and cheese."

"Love it. That sounds perfect." She unwrapped her sandwich and took a bite. "So good." For a little while, they ate in comfortable silence.

"It's been a good day," he said.

"Yeah. It's really coming together. I think Polly is going to love what we've done."

"What *you've* done."

"No. It's been a team effort." She finished her sandwich and wadded up the paper wrapping. "You know what? I was wondering…"

"Uh-oh. No telling what's going on in that non-stop brain of yours."

"Funny. I was wondering if your dad would have enough clippings at the tree lot for us to make a couple more wreaths. We could hang one right over there." She pointed to the middle beam in the shelving unit. "And one opposite, to draw the eye up to some of the items on the higher shelves. Plus, the fresh scent would be so nice."

"Sure. I can make that happen. Why don't I go get them while you're working on this stuff? We can work on the wreaths together later. It would save some time, and we can multi-task."

She stabbed a finger in the air. "I like the way you think."

"I'll see you back here in a little while."

"You've got a date," she said playfully, then rushed over to help Michelle with a box of ceramics someone had just brought in.

Kevin gathered their lunch wrappers and tossed them in the trash, then walked out of the store and got into his truck. As he rounded the corner, he noticed his father's truck in front of the church. In a hurry, he was tempted to ride on past, but he knew needed to make time. He pulled behind Dad's truck and shut down his engine. The least he could do was take a minute to see how things were going. He lifted the door handle and got out. Besides, it was only right to ask Dad if it was okay to take the pine scraps.

Inside the church was quiet. He walked downstairs to the basement.

"Dad?"

Henry popped up from the far side of the bell mechanism. His glasses sat low on his nose, a flashlight in one hand. "I didn't hear you come in."

"Didn't mean to startle you. How's it going?"

"Just like it did every other time I tried to figure this out. I just can't seem to pinpoint what's wrong." His voice was filled with frustration.

"It's not often there's something you can't fix." Kevin realized he was as guilty as his father in not offering kind words often enough. He regretted that now.

Henry's expression softened. "Thanks, son." He lowered his eyes. "I used to believe that was true. These bells have had me stumped for way too long."

"I was hoping maybe the long break would make it like a new start, and you'd figure it out right off." With only two days before Christmas Eve, they were running out of time.

"That would've been nice."

Kevin was so tempted to jump in and start tracing the cogs and cables to see where the breakdown was, but as hard as it was, he refrained from doing so. He didn't want to insult him. Dad wanted these bells to work more than anyone. Of that, he was certain.

"So," Kevin said. "I was wondering if you mind if I run by the farm and pick up some of the tree clippings. Lisa wants to make some fresh wreaths for Daisy's."

"Sure. I'm just going to burn it all."

"That's what I figured. Thanks."

"Have all you want. Or, if you'd rather, you could just take her there and make them. I've got the wire and tools all right there handy. The forms are still in place for the different sizes too. It might be a lot quicker with everything all set up already."

He hadn't considered that. "That's a good idea, Dad. Thanks. I might do that."

Dad leaned over the equipment again. Kevin started to leave, then stopped. "Would you mind if I picked up another tree too?"

"You don't like that other one? They all probably have a flat spot on them."

Kevin regretted judging the tree that his dad had helped Lisa pick out. "No sir. You were right. That one looks great. You should stop by and see it. It's on the front porch. I was going to get her one for inside the store. She really wanted two trees to begin with and I talked her out of it."

Dad's expression softened. "Sure, son. You take whatever you'd like. That Lisa, she's a nice gal. I like her."

"Yeah. Very nice." Kevin walked off, realizing for the first time how much his dad's approval really meant to him.

Chapter Sixteen

Kevin walked back into Daisy's Country Store and it was like nothing he ever imagined. The clutter was beginning to disappear as the shelves filled. It looked nearly ready for business.

Lisa was the only one there. She raised her hands in the air. "Ta-da."

He looked around, slowly clapping as he walked toward her. "Amazing. Definitely standing-ovation worthy."

"Thank you. I couldn't have done any of it without you."

"You're welcome."

She looked past him. "Did you bring the stuff to do the wreaths?"

"Change of plans," he said, rubbing his hands together. "I hope you don't mind."

Her face fell. "Oh. No. Of course not. I understand..."

"No. I don't think you do. We're still going to

make them, but Dad has all the stuff right there at the tree farm to do it. It will be faster, and we won't make a huge mess here."

She lit up. "Oh, yeah. I do love that idea."

"I thought you might," he said. "Temperatures are dropping though, so I thought we could go by the inn, maybe take a little break. I think you could use one. You've been running nonstop all day. While we're at the inn, you can change into some warmer clothes, and then we'll go make the wreaths."

"I don't mind this plan at all. I'm ready." She went behind the counter and got her coat and purse.

"Great. Let's go then." He took her hand and they locked up. "I'll drive."

When they walked into the inn, the aroma of sage from a good country sausage wafted into the hall, making Lisa's stomach growl.

"Something smells good," Kevin said.

"Hey," Megan yelled from the kitchen. "I'm in here. I just made some sausage balls. Come and get 'em while they're hot."

"Don't have to ask me twice." Kevin headed for the kitchen, with Lisa on his heels.

"About time you made it for an evening nosh," Megan teased. "There's egg nog, spiked or plain, hot cider and hot cocoa, and all the usual stuff too. Sweet treats are over on the buffet in the dining room."

"Have you been baking all day?" Lisa lifted a sausage ball to her mouth.

She nodded. "It's been so much fun covering for my sister. I can see why she loves it so much."

"Oh yeah. I can imagine. Meeting new people all the time." Lisa could imagine herself doing something like that.

"We're just going to take a little break, then we'll be heading out again to work on the project."

"Go relax in the den in front of the fireplace. I'll bring you a little smorgasbord of goodies. Sweet and savory."

"Thank you." Lisa followed Kevin into the other room. "This fire is so warm and relaxing."

"It is."

Lisa sat on the floor, and Kevin sat down across from her in front of the fireplace. "Thanks for talking me into a little down time before we go make the wreaths. You're right. We definitely needed this." Her time with him was so easy, and she loved the way he made her laugh.

He reached for her hand, and she laid hers in his. "This is so nice," he said. "I don't know the last time I sat on the floor like this."

"I know. Isn't it crazy? It's the simple things that really resonate, isn't it?"

"Seems so."

"We're a lot alike. Always on the go," she said. "But we both like the simple things too. I guess we need to

173

stop and slow down once in a while too. Kind of even out the pace."

"My dad's always saying I need to slow down." He shrugged. "I've always thought he was a little crazy for saying that, but now I'm not so sure. I think I'm beginning to see what he means."

"Me too. If we don't slow down, we'll keep missing out on this kind of fun." She squeezed his hand. "I like this."

Kevin leaned forward. "I like spending time with you, Lisa. I'm glad you rolled into town like a tumbleweed and swept this town into a frenzy, trying to get that old store back into shipshape. That was no easy undertaking, but somehow, you've got everyone helping. You've created some real energy around Evergreen."

She couldn't believe how happy she was to have stumbled onto this project. It was as if this was something she'd worked her whole life to do. "I wouldn't want to miss this for anything."

"I know how you feel."

After they'd sampled some of Megan's delicious holiday cooking, Kevin slapped his hands against his jeans. "So, Ms. Palmer. Are you ready to go make a couple of wreaths?"

"I most certainly am." She let him help her up, then he got their coats from the coat tree next to the door and waited for her at the door.

"What's next on the big schedule?" Megan asked.

"We're off to make a couple of wreaths, then we're

going to go hang them in the store." Lisa slipped her jacket on. "I'll be back late again tonight."

"No problem." Megan raised a finger. "Wait a second." She disappeared around the corner and came back with a box of ribbons and small ornaments. "These were left over from the wreaths I made. Maybe these supplies will come in handy."

"Thank you." Lisa pushed her hand through the ornaments. "These are great." She ran her fingers down a length of ribbon. "Wire ribbon. You're an angel!" She turned to Kevin. "Wire ribbon is the best invention in the world. A decorator's dream."

"I'm going to take your word for that," he said.

"You two have fun," Megan said.

Kevin took the box from Lisa, and she closed the door behind them.

"It's so cold." She hiked up the collar of her coat and started running for the truck. He passed her and opened the door for her. The heater on the truck was working hard, but it was hardly making a difference against the cold temperatures tonight.

When Lisa and Kevin got to Henry's Tree Lot, there was a nice fire going in the burn barrel.

"At least it'll be warm by the fire."

Lisa clapped her gloved hands together. "Look. There are already two stacks of cuttings sitting here. Fraser and balsam." As she noticed it was exactly what they needed, she eyed him. "Did you do this?"

"Yeah. I got everything ready this afternoon. I

thought it would be a time-saver. We can use all of the time-savers we can get. Right?"

"Right. Thank you." She picked up a few branches and tugged them into an arc. "Have you ever made a wreath?"

"My dad sells Christmas trees. Of course I can make a fresh wreath. In fact, I'm quite good at it. How about I make the wreaths and you decorate them?"

"You've got a deal."

"How big do you want them?"

Lisa shifted from leg to leg and held her hands out, trying to guess the right size. "I'm thinking about a thirty-inch wreath? I know a twenty-four inch is perfect for a standard door, but the store is so big, and with those high ceilings I don't want them to look puny."

"I think you're right. Thirty inches it is."

She started laying small ornaments and pinecones out on the long table and pulling out the wired ribbon she intended to use on each of the wreaths. Not matchy-matchy. The wreaths needed to complement one another, but be totally different. By the time she'd laid everything out and had made one big floppy bow, Kevin was looping a wreath over her head like a beach inner tube and pulling her toward him.

She laughed hysterically as she regained her footing. "Hey! Santa's watching. You better behave or all you'll be getting is coal in your stocking." All kidding aside though, the playful touch had left her reeling in an unexpected and wonderful way.

He pasted an angelic expression on his face and pulled the wreath back over her. "Can't risk that."

"No you can't." She snatched the wreath from him. "Get back to work."

They both worked quickly, tossing the scraps into the burn barrel while families walked by searching for their perfect tree.

While she finished up decorating the second wreath, Kevin helped load a couple of trees.

She walked out to the truck holding the wreaths over her arms. "What do you think?"

"I think you're really good at this."

"It's what I do!"

"That's what I hear." He pulled the keys to the truck out of his pocket. "Ready to head back?"

He put the wreaths in the back of the truck and they drove back.

I'm going to miss making these runs back and forth to the store.

Lisa's alarm sounded at six in the morning. She pushed the snooze button, wishing she could ignore it and stay in bed after being out so late last night.

At least she and Kevin had gotten a lot done. The wreaths were not only made, but hung, plus they'd finished storing away all of the boxes and packing materials. When they left after one this morning, the store was tidy and full. There was still plenty to do though. She pushed herself up to a seated position and planted her feet on the cold wooden floor. She danced around the room trying to find warm socks and jump into her jeans and a sweater. By the time she'd completed the dressing sprint, she was wide awake.

Hopefully, there'd already be coffee brewed. She headed downstairs, stopping every time a stair would creak, hoping she wasn't disturbing the other guests.

"Well hello there." Oliver stood in the kitchen next to the island. He raised his mug in her direction.

"Oliver? What are you doing up so early?"

"It's not early. I'm always up by now. I'm just not always out to all hours of the night like some people. Mmmm hmmm."

He must've heard her come in last night. "Were you waiting up on me?"

"Maybe."

"Then you should be tired, too."

"You're not going to tell me what kept you out to all hours?"

She laughed as she poured her coffee and dropped in a sugar cube. "Kevin and I—"

"How did I know the story would start there?" He leaned his elbows on the counter and grinned. "Go on."

"We drove over to his dad's tree farm and made fresh wreaths for the store. Then we went back to the store and hung them and cleaned the place up. End of story."

"End of story?"

"Well, I don't know." She snuggled up next to him.

"Probably more like the beginning of the story. We work so well together."

"Hey, wait a minute," Oliver said. "Better than you and me?"

"No. Not that kind of work." She waved her hands. "Totally different."

"Okay. Just checking." He pretended to be jealous, but she knew he was just playing.

"He's really nice."

"He's crazy about you," Oliver said.

"Do you really think so?"

"Yes. Don't tell me you can't tell."

"I'm not sure. Sometimes I think so, and sometimes I think it's just wishful thinking."

"Well, keep on wishing. It looks good on you."

"Thank you." She downed her first cup of coffee and poured another. "I can't believe time is flying by so fast."

"I know. Polly will be here Christmas Eve. What do you need me to do?" Oliver's phone buzzed. He picked it up and flipped through his messages. "I have a few things I need to take care of this morning, but I can come over and help all afternoon."

"That would be great. At this point, we have everything we need. It's just a matter of finishing up and perfecting the staging. That's not something other people can really help with."

"You mean making sure everything is slightly askew?"

She laughed. "Yes. That."

"I happen to be an expert at that. I learned from the best."

"Great. I'll see you later then. I'm going to head on over and get started." She grabbed her jacket and purse, then gave him a hug. "Thank you for being here."

"I'm so glad I didn't miss this."

"I know. Daisy's store has been so much fun."

"No, Lisa." Oliver wasn't laughing now. "Not the store. This. Evergreen. You and Kevin. Because I've never seen you this happy. I'm really glad I'm here to see this."

She squeezed his neck. "You're the best bestie in the world."

"I'm going to remind you of that." Oliver waved as she left. "Often. I might even get it tattooed on my arm."

Still smiling when she got to her car, she was thankful he hadn't missed this either. If it weren't for Oliver being here, she might not have acknowledged how she felt, or believed that it was real.

Later that afternoon, the eve before Christmas Eve, it was all hands on deck again. Oliver had shown up and taken the lead on finishing all the things on the main counter. Lisa and Kevin ended up in a pillow fight when a pile of them fell off the display. It was a much longer way to get the job done, but it had been fun.

"Kevin, can you help me scooch this old scale down a little on the counter? It's as heavy as a car."

He rushed over and together they moved it with ease. Lisa had no idea if the antique balance scale was even close to working order, but the turquoise and metal piece was so cool she had to give it a front and center place of honor. As long as she wasn't charging by the pound for anything, that shouldn't be a problem. That scale, maybe dating from the early 1900s, might've weighed anything from babies to gold over the years. More likely candy and nails, but still it was an awesome focal point.

She hung quilted stockings on a wall display and Kevin stacked hand-painted crafted milk-jugs on a shelf. Carol kept the boxes and wrappings cleaned up and stored away.

Nick walked in holding a box.

"Hi, Nick." Carol walked over to him.

"I heard you needed some ornaments," he said, raising the box. Then he held up a red and white antique wind-up car. "And this is for David."

"That's so thoughtful. He and Hannah will be back over in a little while. I'll make sure he gets it."

"I knew you would. It's a bit old-fashioned, but the key to a toy is not how fancy it is, but whether or not it's fun."

"Meanwhile, how about a treat? On the house." Carol lifted a basket of plastic bagged cookies in front of him.

"Don't mind if I do." He peered into the basket,

then plucked a bag from the middle. "Peanut butter. My favorite, but you knew that, didn't you?"

"I did. You're welcome."

"Merry Christmas. I have to get ready for the Festival." Nick rushed off.

Carol waved goodbye to him, and then grabbed another empty box from the counter. "You guys are really whipping this place into shape."

"It's kind of amazing," Lisa said. "Once word got out that we were staging the store with local arts and crafts, people really stepped up."

"I brought some cookies and some of my famous Christmas peppermint bark." Perfectly wrapped in cellophane bags with gorgeous ribbon, she handed it to Lisa. "Figured I'd wrap some up so you could use it to stage the store. Consider it a gift from the Kringle Kitchen."

"Your help is gift enough. Thank you, Carol."

The bell to the store tinkled as Henry walked in.

"Hey, Henry," Carol said. "Merry Christmas."

Henry nodded and walked over to where Lisa and Kevin were standing behind the counter.

Lisa asked, "How are the church bells coming? Please tell me you found a way to get them working and time them so they'll just go off perfectly when Polly comes in the store." *It would be so perfect!*

His smile faded. "Look, I'm sorry, I couldn't get them working." He looked disappointed. "I did all I could, but the system is—"

Kevin's brows pulled together. "Do you want me to take a look?"

Henry lifted his head in frustration.

"Maybe another set of eyes w—"

"You can if you want, but—" Henry raised his hand and let it fall, taking a step back.

Lisa could tell it struck Henry wrong that Kevin offered to look at the bells after him. She looked away. It was hard to see the two of them struggle with their relationship.

"Hey, no. I didn't mean… I'm just trying to—" Kevin took a breath. "Never mind. I'll take a look later."

Henry took a breath. He smiled gently, which Lisa noticed took some effort for him. At least the two of them were trying. He looked around the store.

"You did a good job here." He started to walk out, then turned back. "Both of you."

It wasn't a full out "atta boy," but Lisa appreciated the attempt. "Thank you?" It had come out as more of a question, which she hadn't intended. Trying to lighten the mood, she grabbed a bag of Carol's famous peppermint bark and tossed it to Kevin. "You can have that one."

"Thanks." Kevin dug right in.

Lisa noticed Henry pausing at the door, watching them, with a smile on his face.

There's hope.

Chapter Seventeen

It had been a long day, but the store was ready for Polly's arrival tomorrow. Kevin and Lisa made one last walk through of the place, making sure everything was ready.

"What do you think?" he asked.

She stopped and stood in the middle of the store. "It's beautiful. I think we're as ready as we could ever be."

"Are you ready to call it a day?"

"I am."

"Let me drive you home." Kevin drove her back to Barbara's Country Inn. It had been another great day. He hated to see this project end. She was a little quiet, and he wondered if she was thinking the same thing.

He pulled into the driveway. "I'll walk you to the door."

"You don't have to do that," she said.

"I know. I want to."

"Thanks."

He met her on her side of the truck before she got the door all the way open. He held it, then spotted her as she stepped onto the snowy driveway. They walked toward the house, neither one of them in a hurry.

He'd been trying to find a good time to mention this all night. "Thomas told me he might be opening a new outpost for his logging company here."

Her eyebrows lifted. "Yeah?"

"Yes. So I can choose between staying in Evergreen or moving to Maine." He glanced over hopefully. If she lived here in Evergreen it would be a no-brainer for him.

She slowed down and faced him. "Which way are you leaning?"

"Honestly? I'm not sure." He was bursting inside to just flat-out ask her how she felt. Was there something growing here? It had been a long time since he felt this way and she was so nice, and kind, and thoughtful with everyone. Was it possible he was misreading her and she didn't feel as strongly as he did?

He held her gaze. Then slowly, he reached forward and swept her hair back from her face.

Her lips parted. She licked them, speaking softly. "If I lived here, and I didn't have a business that took me all over the place—"

"And I don't know where I'm going to end up." He shrugged. There were a lot of ifs, but there didn't have to be.

"We might always be in different places."

She drew slightly nearer to him, and the tilt of

her chin seemed like an invitation. He moved in ever so slowly. His heart was pounding, and she wasn't backing away...

Suddenly, the front door of the inn swung open and a man and a woman walked out talking. Kevin and Lisa both jumped back, clearing their throats like two schoolkids getting caught doing something wrong. The two people continued down the sidewalk.

"Excuse me." Lisa stepped out of their path, looking embarrassed, then took a giant step toward the front door. "See you in the morning?" Lisa smiled, not waiting for an answer from him, instead heading for the door.

The moment had passed.

Kevin stood there regretting the timing. It was laughable. He couldn't seem to catch a break. He shoved his hands into his pockets, wishing he could turn back time. "See you then."

He walked back to his truck alone with his heart aching.

The next morning was Christmas Eve. Kevin had barely slept at all, thinking about how he might have made last night end differently. But that was over now. All he had was today.

He'd arrived in town early. There was one last thing he planned to do before he saw Lisa. The 49th Annual Evergreen Christmas Festival banner scrolled between the two sides of the street, but the sun hadn't even come up yet. The town square was still quiet. It wouldn't be that way for long.

He let himself into the store and worked on his secret project. It took him an hour to complete the surprise. He sure hoped Lisa loved it.

His friend Allie would be back from Florida that morning, so he left the red truck on the street in front of the store for her. Then his dad picked him up and gave him a ride home to shower and get dressed for the day's festivities.

When Kevin got back to the town square, he had to park two streets over and walk to the store, which wasn't scheduled to open until noon today. He hoped to arrive before Lisa and maybe get a little time with her alone.

Dressed in a button-down shirt and tie, he walked past the gazebo. Hannah led the children's choir in a round of "Santa Claus Is Coming To Town," and across the way, children lined up to drop off their last-minute letters to Santa in the mailbox.

The festival was in full swing. Booths filled both sides of the streets. There were games and food, and the sound of merriment rose throughout the town.

Kevin spotted Allie standing near the truck. "Hey!"

"Hey." She hugged him. "The latest town gossip is that my truck played matchmaker again."

"Ahh." Word had gotten around fast. He dropped her keys into her hand. "Thank you."

"Thanks for taking such good care of it."

"No problem."

"And by the looks of it…" She pointed to Daisy's Country Store. "the rest of the town."

"No. That was a group effort." He leaned against the front of the truck.

She shook her head. "You know, as long as I've known you, Kevin Miller, you've always underestimated yourself, and covered it up with stubbornness. Trying to make everything perfect."

"All right. All right. I'm aware. How was Florida?"

"We had fun, but it turns out we are Evergreen people. I'm glad to be back in time for the festival, and to help my parents out. Ryan and Zoe will be home tomorrow."

"I'm happy for you, Allie. Ryan seems really great." She'd been lucky to get that chance to have a real relationship with someone she loved. "And now the town has a doctor my dad will actually listen to."

She tossed her head back with a laugh. "That's good. I know how stubborn Henry can be."

"Yeah. He can be." Kevin crossed one boot in front of the other.

"So what's she like?"

He wondered what she'd heard about Lisa. Maybe everything…or more. It was a small town. Gossip was their best crop.

"She's great." He sighed. "But she's probably just passing through."

"Ohh. The curse of the tourist town." Allie nodded. "I've been there."

"I know. Why set yourself up for the heartbreak, right?"

"I'll tell you why." She paused for a moment. "Because you could end up spending Christmas with someone. You know, I may have met Ryan at Christmas, but he only just moved here in August. We're only now figuring it out a year later."

He didn't know how she did it. That would have made him crazy. "So, you're saying—"

"What I'm saying, Kevin, is when the person is right everything is worth it. You make it work."

Lisa was worth it. She was, and if he didn't try he would regret it the rest of his life. And unlike trying again with Dad, there might not be a second chance with Lisa.

How was he going to show her? To convince her that not only was she the right one for him, but that he was the right one for her?

He saw Dad standing in front of the gazebo listening to the carols. This place was special. He and Lisa both belonged here. They could do big things together.

No one that hadn't seen the state of disrepair of Daisy's Country Store a week ago would believe that store had been empty for over a year. They'd done that together. That had to mean something.

There was no time to waste. He left the noise and chaos of the festival and went back to Daisy's. He walked through, checking things over. He noticed a few spots upstairs that could use a little paint touch up. He filled a small paint tray to take care of that while he waited.

He flipped his tie over his shoulder and knelt down to cover a few of the wooden knots that had bled through the first coats of paint. No one would ever notice, but he needed something to do because he was beginning to get nervous. What if she took exception to him putting the tree up in the middle of the store? Yes, it had been her idea all along, but he didn't have her eye or her decorating skills. If she didn't like it there wouldn't be much time to fix it.

He busied himself, becoming increasingly uneasy with her possible reaction to this surprise at the eleventh hour.

Chapter Eighteen

*A*ll dressed up for the festival in a navy dress with a pleated skirt, Lisa took in the sights and sounds as she walked over to the store. Kids squealed with delight as they played "pin the red foam nose on Rudolph" and milk bottle ring toss to win prizes. Over in the gazebo, Hannah led the carolers in a round of ""Jingle Bells"" with such vigor she wondered where someone got that much energy this early in the morning.

Christmas Eve. Polly would be here this afternoon, which was exciting, but the time had flown by and it was sort of anticlimactic that the project was over. She'd made real friendships working on Daisy's Country Store. And there was Kevin. There was something there, and she'd wrestled all night with whether she should be thankful that almost-kiss got interrupted or not.

She walked inside. All the lights were on. Had she been that tired when she left last night? It was definitely possible. The place looked great. She scanned the room. The repairs. The merchandise. Recalling the people that had volunteered to help, and the hiccups along the way, it had been a very good project. She couldn't possibly be any happier with how the store turned out. She'd be proud to show this to anyone.

The pretty white lanterns that they'd placed at the edge of each stair tread looked so nice.

She paused.

In the middle of the store, between the stairs that led to the second level, a floor-to-ceiling tree had been set up.

"Two trees is over-ambitious. We'd run out of time and then it would end up looking sloppy." Those had been Kevin's words. It hadn't been what she wanted to hear at the time, but it was practical and they'd had a long list of projects to complete.

She'd really wanted a second tree, though. She walked a little closer. Pine hung in the air, which made her laugh at the memory of Hannah spritzing the pine spray right before Nancy Redinger had walked into the store. But this wasn't pine spray. That was a real tree sitting in the middle of the store.

She inhaled the scent, closing her eyes and enjoying it.

The huge Fraser fir was only modestly decorated, but it already added that extra life to the room that she'd envisioned. The evergreen picked up the dark green of the industrial light shades hanging throughout the space too.

White lights scattered the full length of the tree, and someone had made an interesting garland out of one of the extra snow fluff blankets they'd used for the village houses. She reached out and touched it. *Not a bad idea.*

She wondered who was behind the surprise. Perched high on top of the tree was the beautiful snow owl she'd seen that first day she and Kevin were in the church, and Hannah had shown her all these awesome things.

Who would have done this? Her mind shied away from the answer her heart wanted. It might've been Oliver, she told herself. It had been his idea to put the partridge on the pear tree at Polly's store in Burlington. But he never would have been able to leave the tree undecorated like this. Not his style. Hannah, maybe?

"Wow."

She spun around. Startled.

Kevin walked forward on the second level. "You look amazing."

A warm glow flowed through her. "Thanks. You do, too." In his dress shirt and tie, with the small paint roller in his hand, he seemed like the perfect answer to any girl's dreams. "What are you doing painting? In a tie?"

"I'm being very careful." He came to the edge of the four-step riser.

"Okay. Good." She glanced over at the tree. "What's this tree about?"

"Yeah. I know I said two trees was overly ambitious."
He came down the stairs. "But, maybe you were right."

"What?"

"I said maybe you were right." He put the paint
tray down. "I'm agreeing with you." He couldn't hold
back the grin as he nodded over and over again. "Is
this a sufficient amount of nodding?"

She nodded, laughing.

"Or do you need more?" he teased with one more
nod.

He was willing to go the extra mile. She didn't mind
that. Smiling, she folded her arms. "I am sufficiently
enjoying this. Yes."

He leaned on the counter in front of some pretty
hand-painted holiday cards by a local artist. "I'm
glad." He knocked on the countertop with his hand.
Inside he was a bundle of nerves.

"Does look good, doesn't it?" She glanced over at
the tree.

"Lucky for us Nick contributed to the cause."
Kevin picked up the small wooden crate of ornaments
Nick had donated. "I was afraid to try to decorate the
whole tree without your help. I also thought it would
be more fun together."

"You're right. Polly's going to be here soon so we
better get started." She took off her coat. "Come on.
Let's do it."

"Yes."

Kevin put the box on the ground in front of the

tree. He picked up a large sequined ball and placed it on the tree.

"These are pretty." Lisa hung a similar ornament on the other side.

"You know, we've been so busy, I realized...I never thanked you."

"Thank me?" Lisa positioned the ball on the tree, then stepped back and peered around the tree at him. "For what?"

He looked to the front of the store. "The town is pretty good at putting these festivals together, but this year, it's a little bit...more magical." He gestured out the window. "Look. My dad is out there talking to a neighbor. I don't know the last time I saw him so at ease and laughing. It's so good to see that."

Lisa smiled.

"And I'm happier. It feels like home here again."

Joy tugged at the corners of her mouth. *It does feel like home.*

He pointed to her. "You did that."

What a nice compliment. It tugged at her heartstrings. "You're welcome." She picked up another ornament. Her voice shook slightly. "So, does this mean you've given more thought to Thomas's offer to stay here instead of going to Maine?"

"I don't know. I mean, I love this town, I just..." Kevin faced her and looked into her eyes. "I'm not sure exactly what's here for me." He looked at the tree, then back at her again.

She pressed her lips together. It wasn't like she

hadn't been thinking about that, too. They decorated in silence until she mustered the courage to ask. "Well, what if there was something here for you? What if… there was somebody who you wanted to spend Christmas with?"

He swallowed hard. "Then yeah."

Her heart pounded so fast she could barely speak. *What comes next?*

He asked, "Are you thinking about it?" Hope filled his eyes.

"Maybe." Nervous laughter overcame her. "Maybe a little." She pushed her hair back over her ear.

He reached out, and she touched his hand as he moved forward and stroked her cheek.

She'd wanted him to kiss her for days now. And the other night. Her mouth went dry. She licked her lips and closed her eyes as she anticipated it.

The bells at the front door tinkled. She gasped and stepped back.

Impossible. Not again! They both straightened and he looked like he was going to laugh as he stood there with his hands on his hips shaking his head.

"Merry Christmas," Michelle said.

"Hey, Merry Christmas," said Kevin, sounding sincere despite the interruption.

"Merry Christmas, Michelle," Lisa echoed.

"I came to look for candles for the processional," Michelle explained.

Lisa pointed toward the back of the store. "Yeah. I actually saw some in there yesterday."

"Of course you did," Michelle said, slapping her hands to her side. "Because Daisy would never let me down."

Lisa felt the same way about Daisy. Probably anyone who'd ever met her did.

Michelle walked past them while Kevin was still holding back his laughter.

After she'd had gone into the back room, Kevin leaned in. "Where were we?"

Lisa's palms dampened. He put both hands on the side of her face. His lips touched hers—

The bells jingled another audible interception. They both pulled back.

"We should consider taking that bell down," Kevin said flatly.

"Yes." She stifled her laugh and tried to look innocent. "Definitely," she said under her breath.

Hannah, David, and Thomas walked in. "Wow," Hannah said. "It looks so good in here, guys."

"Thank you." Lisa tried to sound gracious, but she really wished she'd locked that door.

"Did Michelle come through here?"

"Back room," Kevin said.

Hannah looked to her brother, who headed to the back, amused.

Lisa felt herself blushing. *They can tell.* Had Hannah and Thomas seen them through the front door before they walked in? How embarrassing.

David's eyes widened. "Whoa. Another tree!"

"Yeah," Kevin said.

"Can I help decorate?" David asked.

"Back room," Kevin quickly answered, pointing the way.

Lisa couldn't believe Kevin just said that out loud, although she was thinking it too. She slapped Kevin on the arm laughing. "Yes. Of course you can, sweetheart. You did such a good job on the one out front."

She figured it didn't matter now. The way things were going half the town would be in here within the hour.

Chapter Nineteen

On the back room of Daisy's Country Store, Michelle stood on the stepstool. She tiptoed on one foot trying to reach for a large box on the top shelf in search of the candles she needed for the processional tonight.

"Hey. Are you okay? Do you need some help?" Thomas asked from the doorway.

"No. I just need to look for the..." She moved a box to the right. "Where are they?" She reached into a brown cardboard box in the top corner of the shelf.

Thomas stepped forward to spot her.

"Yes!" She held a candle up. "I found them. They're here." She pulled the long, narrow box from the shelf. "Way to go, Daisy." She stepped down from the stool. "She's still coming through in a pinch." She was pleased to have found them. It would have been hard to find replacements at this late hour.

"Wow," Thomas stood there looking at her. "You really do think of everything."

Michelle laid the single candle back in the top of

the box. "More like over-think. You know I'm a little scared that maybe once you get to know me more that—"

"Hey, listen. None of what you're feeling worries me, Michelle. I get it. You don't think I spend a lot of time worrying and thinking about the complications?"

He was thinking about the same things she was. That was a relief.

"There are still a lot of things to work out if I'm going to expand a logging company down here. It may not happen. I have a son to consider."

"Who's great," Michelle said. "He's funny, he's bright, he's—"

"He's a big fan of yours, too." Thomas looked pleased. "And so am I. I'd like to still keep getting to know you, Michelle. Either way."

He took her hand in his and caressed her fingers. "I like you." Their eyes locked. "I like this."

I like this, too. Michelle took in a deep breath, hoping she wouldn't cry. Her heart was so full right now. She stepped closer and tiptoed to kiss him on the cheek, then walked back out to the front of the store where Hannah and David were both helping to decorate the tree.

"David, I have something for you." Lisa walked over to the counter to get the gift Nick had left for him. "Nick wanted you to have this."

David took the car, and held it in his hands. "Thank you."

Michelle hoped Thomas would explain to him

that there was probably some significant value in that antique tin toy. It appeared to be in mint shape. She looked between father and son standing together now. She could picture herself part of that family. It was as exciting as it was scary to imagine.

David turned the car over in his hands, then looked up at Lisa. "Does it have a remote?"

"No, I don't think it has a remote. It's pretty old. I think they worked a little bit differently back then."

"Cool." He waved the car in the air, steering it down an imaginary highway in the sky. "Thanks."

"You ready to go have some fun?" Thomas asked him.

"Sure. Are you coming with us, Michelle, or are you staying here with Hannah?" David asked.

Michelle's heart warmed at just the fact that he'd asked her to join them. "Thank you so much. I'm going to help Hannah and Lisa until the buyer gets here, but then I'm all yours." Michelle smiled at him. "Deal?"

"Deal!" David and Thomas walked out into the crowd, and Michelle was looking forward to joining them later.

Lisa walked over to the counter where Hannah and Michelle stood. "Before Polly gets here, I just want to thank you all again for everything you've done to help get Daisy's ready for Ezra to sell. Not just for Ezra, but for the whole town."

Michelle nodded agreement. "It's been exciting. I hope this works out."

"We all do," Kevin said.

"We've given it our best effort, and I think it really shows. I'm really proud of how it looks. I just know she's going to love it."

Hannah pointed toward the street outside. "They're here!"

"Oh, my gosh." Lisa rushed around the other side of the counter to greet them.

A hush fell over the room, and a moment later the bells jangled, the front door opened and in walked Polly followed by Ezra, and then Oliver.

It didn't take even one full second for Polly's jaw to drop and sheer joy to spread across her face. "Lisa, this store is absolutely gorgeous!" She threw her hands wide. "I love it." Still bundled in her camel-colored coat, she walked over to the left of the store, her head on a swivel. "Look at these gorgeous pillows. They must've been hand-done." She picked one up, clearly impressed by the quality. She ran her fingers across the tiny button on the fabric wrap of the fragrant goat milk soap. "What a cute touch. I love that."

Polly hadn't even said hello yet, she was so enthralled by the store. A very good sign.

"Beautiful." Polly's excitement was contagious. Lisa's pulse quickened.

"Look at all those nutcrackers. They're all lined up and ready to go," Polly said.

Lisa stood with her new Evergreen friends as Polly

made a turn to see what she'd missed on the right side of the store.

Ezra beamed with pride.

"Oh my goodness, maple syrup, which I love." The Sugar Shack had really come through with a special Christmas batch of maple syrup that had wreaths on the labels. Their display was adorable with their mascots, two chubby squirrels made of buri needles holding acorns. The same person who made the owl on top of the Christmas tree must have made those, too.

"Everything is just…"

It was the first time Lisa had ever known Polly to be at a loss for words.

"Incredible?" Ezra tried to fill in the blanks.

"It's exquisite." Polly said. "It really is." She turned to Oliver. "I love it. The way you mixed the antique items with the new items. Very smart." She wagged a finger toward him and then Lisa.

Michelle quietly moved closer to Lisa, trying not to interrupt Polly's vibe. She put her hand on Lisa's arm and whispered, "Good luck."

Lisa gave her a nod. Michelle and Hannah slid toward the front of the store, smiling back at Lisa and saying quick goodbyes to Ezra as they all filed out.

Kevin started to follow.

Lisa grabbed his arm. "Wait. You're going too?"

"Yeah, listen. Do your thing. Work your magic." He wrapped his hand around her arm. "But…we'll talk later?" He sounded like he was looking forward to it.

"Yes. Definitely." She was looking forward to it too.

Polly went on. "Handcrafted paper? Would you look at that?"

Oliver walked over to stand next to Lisa in front of the Christmas tree. It was the perfect addition to the store. She glanced back at the special surprise. Kevin had done this just for her.

Polly stepped in front of them. "You two have really done it again. It's quaint. It's charming. It has fascinating merchandise." She walked to the back to keep looking. "I just love everything. It's just beautiful."

Ezra stood behind her, nodding with a huge grin. He looked like he was about to burst from the excitement. Lisa was so happy for him.

All the hard work had paid off, and so many people in this town had come together to make it happen. She proudly stood between Oliver and Ezra. "Polly, I can't tell you how much this means to us—"

"And I'm not going to buy it," Polly said matter-of-factly.

Oliver, Lisa, and Ezra all stopped. "What?" The chorus of surprise was followed by silence.

The beads of sweat forming above Ezra's brow made her worry that he might faint. Lisa felt sick. This wasn't what she'd expected, either.

Polly faced Lisa and Oliver. "I came up here with an offer for the both of you. And I wanted to do it in person." She turned and gave Ezra an apologetic nod as she extended her hand. "I'm so sorry to have wasted your time."

Ezra didn't say a word, just heaved a heavy sigh, still staring at Polly in disbelief.

Lisa reached for Ezra, just as Polly began to speak again.

"You have a beautiful store," Polly said, "and I know you won't have any trouble selling it."

"I'll…" Ezra swallowed. "Give you a minute." Crestfallen, he turned toward the door.

Lisa patted his back as he walked away. "I'm sorry," she whispered, then glanced over at Oliver, who was speechless too. She was so disappointed, but Ezra had to feel worse. He'd probably now lose this beautiful store that meant so much to everyone in this town.

"I've come to offer you jobs." Polly lifted her chin.

"What?" Lisa and Oliver shared a confused glance.

"Come work for me. Help me expand, and over time, you'll become part owners. And eventually have your own store."

Oliver looked at Lisa, but Lisa didn't know what to say either. She loved being in business for themselves. Working for Polly, or anyone else, had never been the goal.

Lisa couldn't even believe what was happening. This place seemed perfect for Polly. But not knowing what else to say, she figured the polite thing was to let her continue to explain her offer. "Yes?"

Chapter Twenty

Kevin was deep in thought as he navigated the busy town square. Polly had definitely been impressed with what they'd done with Daisy's. She should have seen it before. He wished now he'd thought to take pictures before they started.

There was no denying the amazing transformation. Even when Daisy was alive it had never looked this good.

As he passed by the Kringle Kitchen, Carol and Joe were handing out cookies to passersby.

"Here you go," Carol said. "I saved a pretty golden-haired angel cookie for you."

He snickered, but graciously thanked her. "I appreciate that." He folded the sheet of wax paper around the cookie and tucked it into his pocket with a smile. There was only one golden-haired angel he was interested in at the moment. That cookie would have to wait.

Nearby, Ezra stood talking to Allie. Everyone was

happy to have her back in town. Her outgoing nature and ever-present smile were Evergreen personified.

As Kevin got closer, Allie patted Ezra on the back. "Hang in there, Ezra. It'll happen next time. It's a great store."

Next time?

Ezra slumped as he walked away.

Kevin intercepted Ezra by the pretzel stand around the corner. "Why the long face?"

He could barely talk. "The store. Polly isn't interested."

"What?" The statement didn't even make sense to Kevin. "That's impossible. I was there. She loved the place. She poured on the compliments."

"Yeah. No denying that, but she said she had no intention of making an offer. She only came to make Lisa and Oliver job offers back in Boston in a new store." He looked back at the store, then hung his head. "I'm sorry I couldn't save it, Daisy."

Pale and glossy-eyed, he met Kevin's eyes again. "I shouldn't have waited so long. I just let too much time slip by before I started to try to sell it."

"Don't do that, Ezra. It is what it is. You did your best, and a lot of people pitched in. It was a valiant effort."

"I'm sorry. I didn't mean to sound unappreciative." He mustered a smile. "I'm so grateful and thankful for everything everyone has done. Especially you. There wouldn't have been a store to stage if you hadn't done the work to get it back in working order to begin with."

He sighed. "I gotta go. I need a minute to pull myself together. I've got a lot of happy, smiling, mayoral duties to take care of here shortly. Excuse me?"

"Of course. Yeah. Sure."

Kevin stood there dumbfounded. They'd worked so hard to get the store ready to sell. Lisa had been so sure that Polly was interested. He was positive she was blown away by the switcheroo, too. Poor Ezra. Losing the store would be hard. He wished the mayor wasn't going through this…but if not for Ezra's awful predicament in the first place, Kevin would've never met Lisa.

But what was Lisa going to do now? A job offer in Boston. It rang awfully close to the conversation he'd overheard between her and Oliver that night.

He looked up just as Lisa, Oliver, and Polly came out of Daisy's Country Store.

His breath caught.

Polly got in her car. As Lisa and Oliver stood there and she slid behind the wheel, Polly said, "The store is lovely. Think about that offer, you two."

That offer. Ezra had said Polly had only come to offer Oliver and Lisa jobs. He stood there watching, unable to move away. *They didn't say no. Boston would change everything.*

"Merry Christmas!" Lisa and Oliver sounded so enthusiastic.

Polly drove off and Oliver clapped his hands together. As soon as she cleared the block, Oliver said,

"We're going to get our own store. Lisa, how many times have we said we wanted that?"

"I know. It's like a dream being handed to us."

Kevin's jaw clamped tight.

"And right there in Boston," Oliver said.

Lisa grabbed Oliver's hands. "We'd be idiots not to take it."

"We would," Oliver agreed.

Kevin's heart sank. *Boston.* He'd heard enough. There was no sense lingering around to talk to her now.

"Merry Christmas, Kevin," someone called from over toward the gazebo.

Kevin looked in that direction. Thomas stood there with Michelle and David. He lifted his chin. "Merry Christmas, guys." He turned back toward Oliver and Lisa. They were hugging and celebrating. Oliver lifted Lisa right off the ground, and then they both ran back toward Daisy's. The sight took his breath.

Through a forced smile, Kevin yelled over the choirs singing to Thomas. "Hey Thomas. I've made my decision."

The choir sang "We Wish You A Merry Christmas" as Kevin gave Thomas the news, and Michelle and David looked on.

They walked down from the gazebo to talk a little easier away from the music.

"This is great news, Kevin." Thomas shook his hand. "I've been waiting so long for someone with your exact experience and qualifications to come along. We're going to take this company to the next level."

"Good deal. I'm looking forward to getting started."

Ezra stepped up to them, waiting for his time to get on stage and make his town announcements.

"Your decision does surprise me, though," Thomas said to Kevin. "Are you sure you don't want to stick around and work from here in Evergreen?"

"Positive. You can plan on me starting the Monday after the holiday." He nodded to Ezra. "Everyone have a merry Christmas. I'm going to get a jump on finding a new place to live in Maine."

"Oh?" Ezra looked confused.

All Kevin wanted to do was get out of there. "Take care," Kevin said. He wandered through the festival with a heavy heart, and then got into his old tan work truck to head to Dad's house to pack his stuff, get out of town and leave all of this behind him.

He cruised around the block one last time. He really didn't care if he never came back to this town again.

As he turned the corner he saw Oliver and Lisa talking with Ezra at the end of the street. They were probably sharing their big news with him.

"Oh, Ezra, I never in a million years expected that to happen. I'm so sorry I got your hopes up," Lisa said.

"It's not your fault," Ezra said. "Don't give that

another thought. I appreciate all you've done. That store has never looked so good. I'm going to ask the bank to come look at it and consider giving me some more time based on all the updates. It's got to be less of a risk for them to carry on their books in the shape it's in now."

"That's great, but there might be one other option." Lisa looked over at Oliver. They both grinned.

"What?" Ezra pointed at the two of them. "What is going on?"

"Polly did offer us jobs, but we counter-offered. Oliver will be managing one of Polly's stores in Boston," Lisa said. "But he'll be doing that as a contractor, still working under our company."

"Oh," Ezra said. "Okay?"

Oliver nodded. "Yes. We're expanding quickly. A whole new service."

"Yes we are. Which also means a pretty nice contract for our company," Lisa said. "One that will give us more money to pursue some of the things that we really want." She looked over at Oliver, then blurted out, "Which is why we would like to buy Daisy's." She raised her hands before he responded. "And we'll run it just like Daisy did."

"What?" Ezra paled. "You want to? Yes. Oh, I accept. Yes, that's amazing." His eyes teared up. "I didn't expect this. Are you staying in town?"

"Yes. I will be," Lisa said. Her whole life seemed to be aligning perfectly. Evergreen. Kevin. And now the store. "I mean, Oliver will be in Boston, of course.

Running Polly's store, but we'll be helping each other, too. What do you think, Ezra? Do we have a deal?"

"Yes! It's a deal." Ezra extended his hand.

She shook it, nearly in tears herself. "Thank you." She never would have imagined her trip to Evergreen would turn out like this.

Ezra shook on it with Oliver too. "Thank you. Thank you both."

"Right on," Oliver said.

Oliver patted Lisa on the back. "Okay. Go find Kevin and tell him."

Ezra stopped her. "Wait. Kevin didn't tell you?"

"Tell me what?"

"He left." Ezra's eyes darted around the festival. "I think he's already gone. He told Thomas he was taking the job in Maine."

"What? When did he do that?" The sun was beginning to set.

"Just a little while ago," Ezra said.

Lisa's chest rose and fell. She looked to Oliver, who only shrugged.

Ezra's phone sounded. "Oh, gosh. I have to go. Mayor duties call. This has been one crazy day. I couldn't have been lower an hour ago. Thank you. Thank you, Lisa, for making this all work out. This is fabulous. You've made my Christmas."

"Bye," she said absentmindedly. "Oliver, why would Kevin have done that?" She'd thought they were in agreement, that they had a plan. She retraced their last discussion in her mind. And the kiss... It just didn't make sense.

She had to find him. "Oliver. I'm going to go look for him."

"Go."

She rushed off. Everywhere she looked there were lights. The whole town was dressed in all its finery for Christmas Eve. Smiling faces, joyful song, twinkle lights and tradition were in full effect. She crossed the town square to Daisy's, where Michelle and another woman were busy relocating Santa's Mailbox to the counter where it originally sat for all those years—near the register. Now it could stay there forever. An important part of the fabric of Evergreen's traditions.

"Merry Christmas Eve, Lisa." Michelle shifted the mailbox into its place.

"Merry Christmas."

"Wait. You're Lisa? I'm Allie," the smiling brunette said. "Apparently we went to kindergarten together."

"Yes." Lisa pointed to Allie. "You wore overalls, and you always talked about puppies."

"Yes!" Allie pointed to Lisa. "And you. Very good with glue. Always kept a clean work space?"

"That was me." Lisa laughed. She hadn't changed much. "That was definitely me. Oh, by the way, I love your truck."

Allie put another small ribbon on the tabletop Christmas tree near the door. "Everyone loves my truck," Allie murmured to Michelle with pride. "How are you finding Evergreen, Lisa?"

"Evergreen is…" She let out a breath. "You know, I thought I'd come here for the holiday, and feel this rush of nostalgia, and get it all out of my system. Then I'd just go back to my own little world."

Allie cocked her head. "But instead?"

Lisa loved this town. That was no exaggeration. "Instead it's like home all over again."

"You're not the first person that's happened to." Allie smiled gently. "Believe me."

Lisa took Kevin's letter from her pocket.

"Mailing a letter to Santa?" Allie asked.

"Ah, no. Actually, this is not my letter. It's Kevin's. Or it was. It was written like twenty-five years ago."

Lisa handed the letter to Michelle.

Michelle took it and tried to explain its significance to Allie. "We found it when we moved the mailbox. This little letter has given us a whole lot to work with this Christmas."

"Yeah. Yeah it has," Lisa said. "It's kind of been like a guide to selling Daisy's."

"Can I read it?" Allie asked.

"Sure." Michelle handed Allie the letter and she stood there reading it as Michelle and Lisa continued to chat.

"Let's just hope everything we're doing works and convinces the buyer to take this place." Michelle looked worried.

"No. Michelle. Polly already left town. She didn't stay for the festival. She didn't make an offer on this place either." Lisa shook her head. "Do you

214

not know?" She'd only just told Ezra, but somehow, she still wouldn't have been surprised if the news had already reached them. "Oliver and I bought Daisy's."

"Wait. What?" Michelle gave a little scream. "You bought this place?"

"Yes!"

"No way! You did. Oh, my goodness." She ran all the way to Lisa and hugged her, both of them jumping up and down. "I was so hoping you would buy it!"

"And I did," Lisa said. "Oliver is going to work for Polly in Boston, but Oliver and I bought this store. Our very first store, and I'm going to stay here and run it."

"I'm so happy about this," Michelle said. "And you're going to stay in Evergreen. This is great."

"Yeah."

"I would have really missed you. I'm so glad you're staying," she said. "Wait a minute." Michelle looked confused. "Kevin told Thomas you bought a store in Boston."

"No." She clenched her fists. *He jumped to conclusions again!* "No. Kevin's got it all wrong. Where is he, anyway? I see his truck out there, and I just... Oh, wait, no." She pointed to Allie. "That's *your* truck."

"Yep." Allie looked up from reading the letter. "Can I just butt in to say I don't think this is Kevin's letter?"

"What? Why would you say that? It's dated. And the initials are K and M," Lisa said.

"Yeah, but all the H's are missing," Allie said. "And Henry always went by his middle name. His first name is Kevin, too."

"What?"

Allie nodded. "I think maybe you guys might be looking at the wrong Miller."

"That makes perfect sense." Kevin had never actually told her he'd written the letter. And he hadn't wanted to talk to his father about it.

"Oliver has my car," she told Allie. "Could you give me a ride? I've got to find Kevin."

Allie leapt into action. "I'll do you one better." She tossed her keys in the air and Lisa caught them. "Take my truck."

Lisa smiled, pleased to get the chance to drive it. "Thank you." She didn't waste another second, racing out to the red truck parked in front of the store.

She hurdled the curb and jumped into the front seat. "Please start." She turned the key and it fired right up. She patted the steering wheel. "Thank goodness." She hoped she remembered the way to Henry's Tree Lot.

Chapter Twenty-One

Michelle tucked the letter back under the mailbox where they'd found it, for safekeeping. So, it was Henry's. That made sense, too. Ruth had always done such a wonderful job with the Christmas Festival. This town still missed her.

Lisa had the same kind of energy Ruth had been blessed with. She brought a breeze of happiness with her wherever she went. People loved to be around her.

Michelle was over the moon that this store now belonged to Lisa. It was the best news. The best Christmas present for Evergreen. Lisa was the perfect person to reopen Daisy's Country Store and carry on the traditions that have made Evergreen extra special for so many years. She had no doubt in her mind that friends and neighbors would frequent the store often, finding joy again in having a single place to shop, share news, and be an active part of the community.

What a crazy holiday this had turned out to be.

Meeting Lisa. And meeting Thomas. Just thinking about him put a smile on her face.

She glanced out the store window and saw him across the way. He wasn't hard to spot, as tall as he was; he stood out in the crowd.

"Allie, can you hold down the fort?"

"Sure."

"Hannah's brother Thomas and his son, David, are in town."

"Do I hear the sound of interest in your voice?" A sly grin spread across Allie's face. "I could see you and Thomas getting along. How cool is that? Are you? Interested, I mean."

Michelle beamed. "Yes. Definitely interested. Allie, he's so nice. I can't wait to tell you all about him."

Her mouth dropped open. "That'll teach me to leave at the holidays. I've missed all the good stuff!" She shooed Michelle out of the store. "Go catch up with him. I've got this."

Michelle pulled on her coat and hurried out the door just as Hannah, David, and Thomas walked up.

"Hey, are you guys having fun at the festival?" Michelle asked.

"Yeah." David waved the key in the air. "I still wish we'd figured out where the key went though, but no luck."

From a distance, Nick called out. "There you are!" He bounded over, fully dressed as Santa Claus.

"Hey, Nick! Merry Christmas!" Michelle said.

"Merry Christmas, everyone!"

David took the old tin car Nick had given him from his pocket. "Thanks for the car, Nick, I really—"

"That's why I was looking for you," Nick said. "On my way here, I reached into my pocket and I found this!" Nick held out the key that winds the car.

"What is that?"

"I forgot to put it in the box with the car. This toy has a wind-up key that makes the mechanism inside it turn." Nick took the red and white car from David, and inserted the key into the slot under the car. He twisted it three times, then handed the key back to David to hold. Then he turned and crouched low, releasing the car and sending it racing down the street with a "Ho-ho-ho."

David ran down the street and picked up the car. As soon as he picked it up, his eyes widened. He held the key in one hand and the car in the other. "Hannah? Are you thinking what I'm thinking?" He turned and looked toward the church.

"I am. I think we've been looking in the wrong place the whole time."

David and Hannah's faces lit up.

"Dad, can I—"

"Yeah," Thomas said. "Yeah. Go!"

Hannah and David ran toward the church. "We'll see you at the festival later," Hannah yelled.

"Okay, we'll see you in a bit," Thomas said.

"We'll catch up with you," Michelle said.

Thomas put his arm around Michelle as they watched David and Hannah rush off, hoping to solve the mystery of that old key. "Come on, Aunt Hannah," David said. They ran directly into the church.

Thomas turned to Nick. "Merry Christmas, Nick. Would you like to walk over to the festival with us?"

"Actually, you two go on ahead," Michelle said. "I'll catch up. I just have one quick thing I want to do."

"Okay. We'll see you in a few."

She watched Thomas and Nick leave. When they cleared the corner, she walked across the street and went inside the Kringle Kitchen. The place was packed and Carol was busy with customers.

Michelle approached the snow globe. The last time she'd picked this up it was to wish for help with this festival a year ago when everything seemed to be falling apart. This wish was much bigger, and much more important.

She looked around to make sure nobody was watching, then picked it up and closed her eyes. She shook the snow globe, and made her wish.

"Please," Michelle whispered.

She gave it one more good shake, and then placed the snow globe carefully back on the counter. She'd wished her heart's true wish. *Work your magic, snow globe.* She left the cafe to catch up with Thomas, hoping for that wish to become a reality.

Chapter Twenty-Two

When Kevin got back to Dad's house, he didn't even remember the drive. He'd been so lost in all that had just happened that he couldn't say whether he'd driven the speed limit, or even stopped at any of the stop signs. Good thing the sheriff and his deputies were all working the festival tonight.

He got out of his truck and slammed the door. The sound echoed through the empty night. He went into the apartment in the barn and grabbed up his clothes and stuffed them back into his duffle bag, then carried it out to the truck.

He wished he'd left when he'd set out to over a week ago. He could have avoided all of this.

As painful as the stings from a swarm of wasps, the rejection hurt at first, but now all he felt was numb. And stupid. Stupid to have thought she'd stay. She'd been upfront with him about how she liked going from town to town wherever her job took her. Why had he expected anything else?

He was thankful that he and Dad had made some positive strides. Hopefully, Dad would have a better Christmas this year. It had always been such a difficult time for them.

He loaded his duffle bag into the bed of his truck. Allie's truck pulled in front of the Christmas tree shed. He hoped she was here to pick up a tree and not to talk to him. He moved on about his business, hoping she wouldn't notice him.

He tied a wide red velvet ribbon around the typewriter, the old Underwood now restored, then carried it to the truck. He nearly stumbled when he saw Lisa get out of the truck and start walking through the snow toward him.

What could she possibly want?

She stopped a good twenty feet away from him. She didn't say anything for a long moment. "You were just going to leave and not say goodbye?"

He stood there holding the heavy typewriter. "I was going to drop off a note."

"Typed?"

"Actually? Yeah." He set the typewriter on the tailgate. "I had it fixed for Dad for Christmas."

"Oh. So the H and the J keys are working."

"Yeah." There was still fifteen feet between them.

"Yeah."

Lisa pointed to the door of Kevin's truck. "K. Henry Miller. KHM."

"Yep."

"Kevin, why did you let me think that was your letter? And not tell me it was your dad's?"

"When I saw the letter, I knew exactly the year that he wrote it. I remember when he dropped it off at Daisy's." It had all come back so fast. He hadn't even had to think about it. "I didn't know what to ask for in a letter to Santa back then. Everything without my mom felt…different. But I didn't want to disappoint my dad so when he said he was going to take me up to Daisy's to drop off my letter to Santa, I went with an empty envelope."

She walked closer.

"I remember showing him the empty envelope with 'To Santa' written in blue crayon across the front. I dropped the envelope in the slot on top of the mailbox and pretended to be excited. I was so sad. I tried to be brave for Dad, but I was distraught. I watched Daisy help a little girl into a big red car with her mom and dad. She looked sad too." He looked away for a moment. "I remember thinking I wished I could have my mom and dad both again."

Her eyes glistened. "Kevin. I'm so sorry."

"And then I went over to look at the toys, but out of the corner of my eye I saw my dad put a letter in the mailbox. I never knew what it said. Until now." He shook his head. "Not until you gave me that letter. It answered so many questions for me. My dad was so quiet after Mom died, and I was so sad. I never saw him cry. I often wondered if he felt anything. If he missed her at all."

Kevin and Lisa looked at each other, standing there under the dark sky and bright stars.

Lisa's expression softened. "I remember you that night."

"Do you think we were there at the same time? I've been wondering this whole time if that little girl was you."

"It seems impossible, but I've wondered that too. That night I was wishing I could stay, but I'm still confused," Lisa said. "So you did all this with the store and the festival because of the letter?"

"No. I did all of this because of you." His voice was full of pain. "You swept in here and for the first time in a long, long while, I'd gotten back a piece of what Christmas used to be."

Lisa's heart seemed to flood, lifting the darkness that had settled there on the drive over.

"When I read that letter, and realized it was from my dad, that was even more reason, but it was you all along. That letter seemed like proof that I was doing the right thing. On the right path."

Henry walked out from the corner of the building. "This was all your doing, son?"

Kevin turned to face his dad. "Dad?"

He walked over to them, stopping by the truck to look at the typewriter. "I wrote that letter twenty-five years ago. When the townspeople…they brought your mother back in a way by carrying on her traditions… preparing the candlelight procession and the choir."

"I just wanted you to have what you asked for in

the letter." Kevin stepped up to his father. Tears choked him. He hadn't felt this close to his father since his mother had died.

Henry pulled him into a tight hug. "You did, son." A tear ran down Henry's cheek as they hugged for a long moment. He released him from the embrace and patted his shoulder. "You did," he repeated, looking Kevin right in the eye. Then he patted him on the back and turned to Lisa. "You both did."

Lisa was crying, too. She ran to Henry.

"Thank you," Henry said. "You're the best part about this Christmas. You brought a lot of joy to a lot of people."

"Thank you." Lisa hugged him and then stepped back, looking toward the heavens just as snowflakes began to fall. She instinctively held out her hands to catch them.

Back in town, at that moment, Hannah and David stood in the basement of the Evergreen Church where the mechanism for the church bells was housed. With a whole new lens on things, they looked for a slot where the key might fit. It wasn't easy. The mechanism was a maze of cogs and wheels.

Finally, at the same time, they spotted it.

There on the side of the metal housing was a simple keyhole. It wasn't labeled. It wasn't anything special at all, but the big slot was about the size and shape of that special key.

David raised the key in anticipation and Hannah hurried him along. They raced closer and David slid the key into the slot. It fit easily.

He glanced at Hannah and she nodded, encouraging him to turn the key.

David closed his eyes, held his breath and with all of his strength he turned the key one strong half turn. The cogs clunked as they made a single turn. The thick ropes slightly shimmied in front of them.

Hannah and David stared at each other.

She reached over and tugged on the rope. The rope pulled freely, sending one clapper against a bell at the top of the tower. *Bong.*

They both gasped as the sound echoed around them. Their hands flew to their ears as that single tone continued to reverberate.

Hannah and David looked up into the bell tower in awe.

"It worked, Hannah!"

It was 11:59. One minute before Christmas, and Hannah and David had no idea what was getting ready to happen.

When the big hand jumped straight up to the twelve with a click, the ropes began to move up and down in a slow rhythmic motion.

Not just one bell, but each of the seven bells rang out. The four stationary ones and the three that swung independently sent a beautiful vibrating noise out to the world—so loud that it tickled their teeth and throbbed in their ears.

They both clapped their hands over their ears.

"We figured it out!" They jumped up and down in delight, nearly disoriented by the striking harmonic tones of the bells.

Hannah grabbed David's hand and ran outside.

Chapter Twenty-Three

$\mathcal{I}$n town, the noise of the bustling festival filled the air. Michelle handed Allie a candle, then handed candles to Megan, Joe, and Carol. "Merry Christmas." She looked around, trying to piece together what she was hearing. Others stopped and looked too. Then, the carolers stopped. The ringing continued. Strong and rich.

Michelle stood there, stunned. "Are those...the church bells?"

Looking up at the church bell tower, the clock's hands were straight up, and the bells—the bells that hadn't rung in so many years—were now joyfully swinging.

Some townspeople paused in amazement; others, who had been stuffing their faces with holiday treats, stopped mid-chomp. As the chatter quieted, only the sound of those bells could be heard, ringing out over the town.

People looked at one another—some with delight

at the memories those bells held. Some were just confused. They held their lit candles and began to line up for the midnight processional in awe of what was happening.

Snow began falling in huge flakes.

Nick, wearing his Santa outfit, sat on Santa's sleigh looking up at the sky and smiling at the sound of the bells, and the smiles on all of the faces.

All around, the Christmas Festival had been in full swing, but now a hush fell over it. Only those bells broke the silence of the night.

People huddled in delight, smiling.

Michelle made her way through the crowd with the nearly empty box of processional candles in her arms. "Here. Merry Christmas."

She handed out the last of the candles as she headed toward the church, still not quite believing that they'd somehow pulled it off. The biggest miracle of all.

The townspeople moved down the road, getting in line with their candles lit, ready for the special walk.

Michelle's eyes blurred from the tears of joy the sound from those bells had given her. Her heart was full this Christmas…in so many ways. *It's just like the processional used to be. And it's a glorious thing to behold.*

As far off as Henry's farm, clear off on the outskirts of town, the sound of those church bells filled the night.

Henry, Kevin, and Lisa stood there looking at each other.

"Is that the bells?" Lisa asked.

Kevin broke into a smile. "Yeah!"

She laid her head against his chest, laughing. "This is truly magical."

Henry nearly stumbled at the realization of what that sound was. Kevin reached for his dad, and hugged an arm around him. They all stood there for a long moment, just taking in the crisp powerful notes.

Now everything in the letter had been satisfied. The carolers, the bells, and now that it was midnight everyone in town would be lining up for the candlelight processional.

We can't miss this. Lisa grabbed Kevin's hand. "Come on."

He let her drag him along, but he turned back to yell, "Come on, Dad."

They piled into Allie's truck and headed to town. Lisa sat in the middle, between Henry and Kevin.

"Roll down the windows so we can hear the bells!" she said.

None of them even cared that the night air was as frigid as the Arctic. "It's glorious," Henry said with a hearty laugh.

She wrapped her hands around Kevin's bicep, hugging close against him. Not only because of the cold, but because this moment was one she would cherish with him forever.

He drove fast, but safely straight back to town. Rather than finding a parking spot, he parked on the street in front of Daisy's and all three of them hopped out of the truck.

They stood in the middle of the street looking up at the church, the steeple, and those bells swinging as freely as if they had always been able to.

"Merry Christmas, Ruthie," Henry said.

Lisa looked toward the heavens. "You too, Daisy."

Kevin put a hand on his father's shoulder. Missing his mother, but so grateful for the beginning of a new, softer relationship with Dad, and for Lisa. He wished Mom were here to see this: all they'd done, with her at the core of it.

He looked over at Lisa. Without her, he may have never found this peace with Dad.

Henry moved toward the church to catch up with the lit candle processional.

A single angelic voice from the choir sang the sweetest Christmas song in the entire world. "Silent Night" carried across the loving people of Evergreen as they carried their candles.

People moved slowly, in no hurry for it to end.

All is calm. All is bright.

With the bell tower now operational, the angels—who had once worked their way in a circle below the clock, but had been frozen like statues for so many years—now moved again, each taking their turn to see the town.

David and Hannah came out of the church and looked surprised by the snow.

"It's beautiful," David said.

He and Hannah caught up to the processional as it moved toward them from downtown. Henry handed him a candle. "Merry Christmas, David."

The processional of candles wound its way through town and to the church, with Michelle, Thomas, Allie, Megan, Ezra, and Joe and Carol, all leading the way.

Thomas stepped out of the processional with Michelle, both taking a moment to enjoy the sight. She laid her head on his shoulder.

"This place," Thomas said looking into Michelle's eyes. "It's magical."

"You should see it during the other seasons." How she wished he could.

He smiled gently. "Looks like I'm going to."

She turned, hoping he wasn't kidding.

"We'll be opening another location down here over the summer."

Hope filled her heart. She snuggled up against him, so excited to see what the year might bring them.

Thomas took Michelle's hand. Lisa and Kevin smiled knowingly at one another. Something very special was happening right now.

The bells added to the glorious voice of the singers, and the joy of the moment.

Still looking to the sky, Lisa took Kevin's hand in hers. "We didn't take the job in Boston."

He cut his eyes toward her. "You...?"

She turned and faced him. "We bought Daisy's. I'm staying here."

He let out a breath. "I guess I should've gotten the whole story before—"

Lisa kissed him before he could finish.

Kevin wrapped his arms around her, and pulled her closer.

The kiss was finally happening. No interruptions this time.

For a moment she was lost in time and the world seemed to fall away.

Thomas's voice came from across the way. "So I guess you'll be joining me at the new location, Kevin."

Lisa laughed as she kissed Kevin. No, it would have been too perfect if they hadn't been interrupted. But this was for good reason.

She didn't even bother to step away.

He never took his eyes off of her. "Yeah," he said breathless. He glanced over at Thomas. "Can we shake on it later?" Without hesitation, he kissed Lisa again.

As if it had all been planned, the choir led the entire processional in "We Wish You A Merry Christmas."

This was, most certainly, her merriest Christmas ever.

Everyone held their lit candles, with eyes still cast upon the ringing bells and singing.

"Lisa! The key!" David pointed to the bells. "It was for the bells."

"How'd you figure that out?"

"I realized that if I added up everything Nick said, it pointed to the church."

Kevin placed a hand on David's arm and gave him a nod of approval for the good problem solving.

"This is the best Christmas," David exclaimed. "I don't how anyone will ever top this Christmas Festival."

Henry walked up behind David and placed a hand on the young boy's shoulder. "That's just it, David. We don't have to top it. This is Evergreen's tradition. It's perfect just the way it is."

"Christmas like it used to be." Henry cuffed Kevin's shoulder. "Thank you, son" He nodded toward Lisa. "Thank you both." Tears glistened in his eyes.

Lisa turned to face Kevin. "Merry Christmas, Kevin."

He took both of her hands into his. Yes, this was Christmas like it used to be. His heart was full, and he could see more than just work on his path now. Lisa had walked right into his life at just the right time. "Merry Christmas, Lisa." He kissed her again as the snow fell down upon the town, and the whole town gathered in songs of praise.

And so, once again, the town of Evergreen celebrated Christmas like they used to...all the while remembering that keeping family and friends close is the greatest Evergreen tradition of them all.

Epilogue
Six Months Later

$\mathcal{L}$isa stood on the sidewalk in front of her store looking up at the sign. Dressed in her favorite sundress—the one with daisies on it, of course—she tipped her face to the sun. Warmth washed across her.

It was hard to believe she'd owned Daisy's for six months now. It seemed as if every job she'd had before had prepared her for this. She'd been worried about settling down in one spot, that she might miss the travel, but she hadn't. Not one bit. Of course, she and Oliver still did their quarterly merchandising trip, and now that was even more exciting since they were buying inventory for their own stores.

I have the best job in the world.

She waved to a neighboring merchant as he opened his doors for the day too. It was a perfect summer day. Too pretty of a day to spend inside. She rolled a three-tier rack out onto the sidewalk for an impromptu sale, and started moving merchandise out on it.

"Hi, Lisa!"

Lisa spun around to see Michelle and David, followed by Allie and Ryan's daughter, Zoe, filing out of the Kringle Kitchen.

"Hey!" Lisa waved. "Where are you headed this morning?"

"I'm on my way to work," Allie said. "Michelle is taking David and Zoe to the library to sign up for the summer reading program."

"Awesome." Lisa gave them a thumbs up. "Have fun."

Lisa rearranged the items and made sale tags. It was perfect timing to make room for the new things that would start coming in next week. She placed a daisy-shaped sign in the center of the table and updated the chalkboard slat with the message, "50% Off."

Inside, two high school girls helped customers and worked the register.

"I can't believe I lucked out with this pretty weather on my one day off this week." Hannah walked toward her on the sidewalk with her pug, Molly, on a bright red leash.

"Good morning, Hannah." Lisa crouched to pet the puffing pug. "How are you doing, you sweet thing?"

Molly tilted her head, her little pink tongue curling with each pant.

"We have an appointment for Molly to see Allie." Hannah pointed across the street to Dr. Allie Shaw's

Evergreen Veterinarian Clinic. "It's time for Molly's shots."

"Tell Allie and Michelle that the four of us need to get together soon. We've been talking about it for weeks."

"You're right. Everyone's so busy. We just need to make it happen," Hannah agreed. "How about Saturday night? Six o'clock. We can get together at my house. I'll throw something on the grill."

"That sounds perfect. Tell Allie to clear her calendar for a relaxing girls' night."

"I will. I better hurry or I'll be late. Right after this, I'm meeting with a couple at the church about the music for their wedding."

"I'd heard Evergreen was a wedding destination, but I had no idea just how big of a business it was here until recently." Lisa glanced over at the Kringle Kitchen sign. It was too funny to see Santa in beach britches. It made her laugh every time she looked across the street. Visitors seemed to love it though. "I've been thinking about adding some wedding themed items to my inventory."

Lisa had been thinking a lot about weddings lately, and not just from the perspective of buying for the store. A year ago she'd pretty much decided settling down and getting married wasn't in her future, but now she'd put down roots in Evergreen, and she could picture herself in a long, white, lacy veil with Kevin in her life.

"Oh yeah. June and July are non-stop weddings

around here. Wedding party gifts would be good too. I was talking to Gladys over at the new flower shop. She said business was better than she'd ever dreamed."

Lisa nodded. "I bet. People are coming and going all day over there." Kevin had been one of Gladys's first customers, placing an order for a fresh bouquet to be delivered every Saturday morning to Daisy's for her counter. It had been such a thoughtful gift. One she'd really enjoyed. "I love seeing our small businesses thrive."

"Me too. We have to go. I'll talk to you later." Hannah waved as she walked across the street to Allie's veterinary clinic.

The new flower shop had just opened last month in the space next to the bakery. The small building had once been the dentist's office, before they outgrew it, and then the clock shop before old Mr. Tynsdale retired. Finally, every storefront in the square was filled and thriving.

Ezra had done the ribbon cutting for Hannah's brother's business, Branford Logging, just last month too, although it was located on the outskirts of town. Kevin had settled in to his job there with Thomas, and it seemed as if business was booming in Evergreen on all fronts.

Lisa was inside ringing up a customer when Hannah walked back by with Molly on her leash. She poked her head in the door. "We're on for Saturday night."

"Awesome. I'll bring potato salad."

"See you then."

That evening Kevin met Lisa at her house with a grocery sack in his arms.

"I take it we're eating in tonight," she said.

"Yep. I'm cooking for you."

"Nice." She loved that he was as good in the kitchen as he was fixing things.

He whisked past her, making himself at home. As he unloaded the bag, her stomach growled.

He whipped around. "Sounds like I got here just in the nick of time."

"I know. Right?" She rubbed her stomach. "I haven't eaten all day. I had a steady stream of customers. The first time I checked my watch it was almost closing time."

"That's great. Seems like things are staying steady." He leaned over and gave her a kiss. "Daisy would be proud with all you've done."

"Thank you, Kevin." She sat down in one of the chairs and watched him chop vegetables and prepare dinner. Her role was always just to keep him company, which she liked to think she excelled in.

He opened a bottle of red wine and handed her a glass. "To us," he said. "I'm so thankful Daisy brought us together. My life has never felt so complete."

She tipped her glass towards his. "Me too." She took a sip of her wine, and watched him as he turned back to dinner.

"Do you think we would have ever gotten together if Thomas hadn't offered you that job here in

Evergreen?" It was a loaded question. She knew it as soon as it came out of her mouth.

He kind of laughed, looking at her like he wasn't sure how to answer. But she loved the ways those lines formed around his eyes when he smiled like that. "I think, Lisa, that somehow we'd have eventually ended up together. It just seems meant to be."

She nodded.

"And Dad," Kevin said. "Man, you've made a new man out of him."

"That's not my doing. Uh-uh." She waved her finger toward him. "Your relationship together has just gotten easier. It's been good for both of you."

"Because of you. Thank you for that."

"He's a good man. Like you."

"Thank you. But you know, I'm thankful Thomas opened the new branch. It's been good for everyone in Evergreen, bringing other jobs and revenue to town too. I hired two more locals this morning, plus the apprenticeship program was approved today."

"Really? That's great."

He looked proud. "Michelle was a big help with that. We got it approved for five students this year, but if things go well, we can expand it each year. I think this can be really great."

She set her wine glass down, walked over and hugged him. "I'm so proud of you."

"It wouldn't mean nearly as much without you." He dropped a kiss on the tip of her nose. "Hey, how about we celebrate tomorrow night? I'll take you to Burlington for a special night out. Somewhere fancy."

A smile that started in her heart spread across her face. How did I get so lucky? Kevin was always coming up with thoughtful ideas from as small as bringing a dandelion over to blow and share a wish, Scrabble night at the community center, or going to the city for a fancy meal. "As wonderful as that sounds, I just made plans with the girls for tomorrow night. We're meeting up at Hannah's. Just girl stuff."

He pouted, then playfully pulled her closer. "I'll take a rain check then."

"You got it."

On Saturday morning, Hannah walked into Daisy's with a young blonde woman who looked like she'd been crying.

"Good morning." Lisa flashed a questioning look to Hannah.

Hannah led the girl to the counter. "This is Amy. She's the bride that I met with that I was telling you about yesterday."

"Oh, that's great. Congratulations. Yes. So nice to meet you." Lisa looked at the young lady. "You're in for some treat. My friend here, she sings like an angel."

"She is an angel. I'm so glad she's going to help us out. Evergreen is the best," Amy gushed.

"We need your help too," Hannah said to Lisa.

"Mine? Oh, do you need wedding party gifts? Last minute something for the groom? I have—"

"No." Hannah interjected. "She needs something a little more personal."

Lisa wasn't quite sure what that meant.

Hannah nodded, encouraging Amy.

After a long pause, Amy grimaced and then blurted out, "I need bridesmaids." She pressed her hands over her face. "This is so embarrassing." She dropped her hands and took a deep breath. "I already have the dresses and flowers. Everything. Please? The wedding is tonight."

"Excuse me?" She couldn't have heard her right.

The girl's eyes pooled.

Hannah squeezed Amy's hand. "It's kind of complicated, but Amy and her fiancé are supposed to get married tonight. His family has never met her, and they've been quite judgey about the small wedding."

"I've always pictured a small wedding," Amy said. "It's all I've ever wanted."

"I don't blame you," Lisa said. "This is something special between you and him and those closest to you."

"That's exactly how we felt, and I know it's not all that popular of an opinion, but I don't see the need to pay thousands and thousands of dollars for a big fancy wedding. That day is just the first of the rest of our lives together."

"Right."

"At the insistence of his mother, I finally gave in to having a bridesmaid, which ended up being three.

She even picked out and paid for the dresses." Amy's words trailed off.

Lisa wondered what kind of woman would treat her son's fiancée that way. She also wondered what those dresses looked like. They could either be really spectacular, or if she was doing it out of spite…a spectacle.

Hannah picked up where Amy left off. "Anyway, Amy's three girlfriends were going to drive here from Memphis, only they've had car trouble on the way and they are not going to make it. I was there when they called."

Amy swallowed. "This would be all the excuse his mom would need to try to make us wait. Hannah thought maybe since my new in-laws don't even know the girls maybe we could get someone else to stand in as the bridesmaids, and let the wedding go on."

"I understand, but starting out your wedding on a lie?" Lisa wasn't so sure that was a good idea either.

"I'm not lying to my fiancé. We're just pacifying his mother. His parents are leaving right after the ceremony. This morning they called right before they left to come here and offered him twenty-five thousand dollars if he canceled the wedding."

"That's awful. Are you sure you want to marry this guy? His parents are always going to be in the picture."

"I know, but he's a good man. He's truly my soul mate. We're so good together. I know all of this sounds crazy and it's so much to ask, but…"

Lisa's lips drew into a tight line. "What if the dresses don't fit?"

Hannah grinned. "I saw them earlier. Even tried one on. I can wear it. I think you and Allie will fit perfectly in them too. If they're too big I can do enough of a tack and pin to get us through a thirty-minute wedding. Tonight at 8pm. Sunset ceremony in the gazebo."

Lisa was dying to ask what those dresses looked like, but that was not the point. What was important was this girl's wedding day. "It'll be beautiful. Sunset weddings are so pretty and the way the sun sets over the gazebo here..." She looked at Amy, putting herself in her shoes for a moment. "It's going to be breathtaking. You'll be breathtaking. But Hannah, we had plans with Allie—"

"I know. But I think we should do this instead. We can make it fun. It'll still be a girls' night out. We'll just be dressing up. I already asked Michelle to come do our hair and makeup. We'll get dressed at my house, and then go to the church."

"What did Allie think about all of this?"

Hannah's nose crinkled. "She doesn't exactly know."

"When are you going to spring it on her?"

"When she gets to my house at six."

Lisa laughed. "How can she say no?"

"She can't. That's what I'm counting on."

"What if she does say no?" Amy wrung her hands.

"She won't. Come on. How could any of us say no

to something as romantic as helping a girl marry her soul mate?" Hannah hugged Amy.

"That's true."

Hannah turned to the bride-to-be. "See. I told you. No problem. Disaster averted."

Lisa should've known when Hannah didn't bring those dresses out when they first got to her house that it was bad news.

Allie took one look at the bright orange gown and said, "I knew I should've said I had to leave to take Frank out for a walk."

"Frank?" Lisa looked at Allie and then Hannah. "Who's Frank?"

Hannah put a hand on her hip. "Her goldfish. The one in the bowl on the counter in her office. Allie, it isn't that bad."

"It's not that good, either." She lifted one of the poufy orange dresses and held it up against her.

"I have to agree." She started laughing so hard that she snorted, which only made all of them laugh.

Michelle stood there with her arms folded. "I am going to promise all three of you right now that if Thomas asks me to marry him—"

"When he asks," Hannah interrupted.

Michelle crossed her fingers. "I promise I will not dress you in orange. Or ruffles."

Allie sucked in a breath and smoothed the dress. "Thank you for doing our hair and makeup, Michelle, although under the reflection of all this orange I'm not sure anyone will see it."

"Stop it. You girls are beautiful. You could wear feed sacks and look pretty. Now, let's get to the church so we can get this girl married and get back into our blue jeans."

They piled into Michelle's car, and she drove them over to the church.

At eight o'clock, Hannah, Allie, and Lisa stood inside the church with the nervous bride. From here they'd walk to the gazebo where the groom, his brothers and the preacher all stood waiting.

The wedding march started outside and Michelle opened the door. "Here we go."

Hannah started out the door and down the path toward the gazebo. Since she'd be singing, she stepped off to the left and up next to the organist. Lisa and Allie walked out next. Then those famous notes rang out and everyone stood, waiting to see the bride.

Amy stepped between the tall open doors of the church. Her simple white gown swept the ground around her as she started toward the gazebo.

Lisa watched the groom's mouth drop open with Amy's first step, and then a smile spread across his face. He loved her. There was no denying that.

His parents stood in the first row. His father looked proud, but his mother wore a lovely Chanel dress and a tense, crooked half-smile. Lisa was pretty sure the hideous dresses were not an accident. She held her shoulders back, determined to wear that dress like it was a coveted designer number.

As Amy approached the gazebo, Lisa stepped forward to help with her dress as she stepped next to her husband-to-be. There was no giving away of the bride in this ceremony. Amy's parents lived in Seattle and for health reasons couldn't make the trip.

Lisa took the bride's bouquet and held it, along with her smaller nosegay of bright orange gerbera daisies and white roses.

The ceremony was simple, with the standard words, although Lisa noted there had been no objection clause mentioned. Probably for the best, based on Amy's future mother-in-law's expression.

After the I-do's, but before the kiss, the organist began playing. Hannah sang.

Lisa gulped back tears while listening to the beautiful lyrics and picturing herself in this very position one day. The love in the looks between the bride and groom was undeniable. Her heart filled, brimming over.

Hannah finished singing and stepped next to Allie, who squeezed her hand. "Beautiful," she whispered.

The preacher paused just a moment, then looked to the groom. "You may now kiss the bride."

Robert laid a joyful kiss on Amy, and then the preacher turned them to face the guests. "I'd like to now introduce to you, Mr. and Mrs. Robert Hayes."

The wedding party followed the bride and groom to receive the guests.

Amy and her husband stood at the front of the receiving line. Allie, Hannah, and Lisa said hello and shook hands as if they'd been friends with Amy forever.

Just as Amy had said, the groom's parents said their congratulations and then left, not even spending one extra moment for a picture or to grab a little something to eat.

"That is the most bizarre thing I've ever seen," Lisa whispered to Michelle. "I can't believe they left like that."

"Different people with different priorities. That's what makes the world go 'round."

"I guess."

Amy walked over with a thousand-watt smile. "I'll never be able to thank you enough."

"Just be happy," Lisa said.

"And come back to Evergreen to celebrate your anniversary!" Michelle added.

"Or anytime," Lisa said. "You should see Evergreen at Christmas."

Amy grabbed for Robert's hand. "We're so grateful for your help."

Robert's cheeks reddened. "My mom will come around. She can be hardheaded when she doesn't get her way. Thanks for not letting her ruin our special day."

"You're welcome," the ladies said.

"It'll be a fun story to tell our grandchildren someday," Hannah added.

"All kidding aside, this has turned out to be kind of fun." Lisa lifted her flowers. "I'm also totally stealing this daisy nosegay idea for my bridesmaids."

"No offense," Allie said to Amy, "but Lisa, there better not be orange involved or you can count me out."

"No offense taken," Amy said. "I cried when those dresses arrived and I opened the box."

"I bet." Lisa shook her head. "Out of all of us, only Hannah seems to be able to pull off orange."

She curtsied. "Thank you very much."

"And your singing," the groom said. "It was beautiful. This has been the best day of my life."

Amy wiggled her fingers, letting the shiny band of diamonds cast rainbows around them.

From here they could see the musicians already loading their equipment into the gazebo and hooking up to the sound system.

"I hope you're all planning on staying for the reception," Robert said.

The four of them looked to one another. "We hadn't."

"You should." Amy and Robert pleaded. "Please stay."

"We're all dressed up with no place to go." Lisa shrugged. "Might as well."

They mingled and noshed, toasting the bride and groom with very nice champagne.

From the gazebo a band played a nice mix of oldies and contemporary music while the guests danced under the stars.

When Amy and Robert cut their cake, there was no messy cake smashing. Just a polite, loving exchange.

Lisa nudged Hannah. "I'm not sure I'd get off that easy with Kevin."

"I was just thinking the very same thing," Hannah said.

Michelle flashed a concerned look toward Hannah. "Oh, Thomas better know better."

Allie rolled her eyes. "None of them know better. Let's get some cake. It looks like it's chocolate, and I'm starving."

Lisa took a piece, and for a moment imagined her own wedding, swaying to the music as she took a bite of the sweet confection.

"This has turned into a very fun night," Hannah said. "I might be tempted to turn into a permanent wedding crasher."

Lisa shook her head. "I have a feeling we wouldn't be very popular."

"I don't think putting one of our best tourism angles at risk is a good plan, but this has been fun," Allie said.

Hannah spun around with her fork in the air like a fairy godmother ready to grant a wish. "The question is, which of you will be the next to get married, so we can do this again?" She raised her eyebrows. "All of you have special guys now."

Allie, Lisa, and Michelle all swapped looks.

"We need all the single ladies over here," blasted through the speakers. "It's time for the bride to toss her bouquet."

Lisa, Allie, Hannah, and Michelle hung back, watching the other wedding guests rush to the makeshift dance floor for the big moment.

Then over the microphone, he announced, "Hey bridesmaids, we need you over here too."

They all shook their heads. "We're good," Lisa called out.

"All the single ladies," he said. "Looks like they need some coaxing," he roared over the mic. The drummer pounded out a drum roll and the party-goers all clapped and urged them.

"We can't just leave Amy hanging like this," Hannah said. "Come on. No one says we have to actually try to catch the bouquet."

"True," Lisa said. "Come on. Let's go."

They rushed over and joined the group of excited women.

Amy faced them. "I hope whoever catches this bouquet will marry a man as wonderful as my Robert, and will be as happy as I know we'll be." She turned her back on them and chucked her bouquet high over her head into the center of the group of ladies.

Arms flew in the air, and a gal wearing bright purple literally dove horizontally past Lisa in an attempt to catch it.

Michelle shielded her face, and Allie squealed as

the flowers headed right for her like a softball hit to right field. Allie's athletic instincts took over and she caught the flowers.

"Whoa." Lisa was shocked. "Oh my gosh!"

Hannah jumped up and down, laughing.

Allie's eyes were wide, realizing what had just happened.

Then Michelle pointed across the street. "Look!"

Outside of the Kringle Kitchen, Thomas, Kevin, and Ryan all stood staring at them.

"I think we've got some explaining to do." Lisa smoothed her hands down the front of the hideous bright orange dress. "Last I talked to Kevin, we were grilling out at Hannah's." She offered a tentative wave in his direction. Kevin smiled and lifted his chin, then gave her a flirty wolf whistle.

"Funny," she said with an eye roll.

Ryan cupped his hands to his mouth. "That looks good on you, Allie."

"I hope he means the bouquet and not this dress," Allie said.

"Was that a proposal?" Hannah asked.

Allie looked at the bouquet in her hands.

"I think it might have been the precursor to one," Lisa said. "And here they come."

"Oh, my gosh." Hannah laid her hand on her heart. "An Evergreen couple getting married in Evergreen. We're long overdue for one of those."

"An Evergreen wedding." Michelle sucked in a breath. "That sounds really good to me."

Kevin was the first one to make it across the street. "Hey pretty lady," he said to Lisa. "So, this is what girls do on girls' night?"

Lisa shook her head, glancing at Hannah with a nervous giggle. "We can explain."

Hannah's eyes widened. Then she said, "Always a bridesmaid, never a bride?"

Kevin leveled a stare toward Lisa. "That's easy to fix, you know."

Lisa's mouth dropped open, then she snapped it shut with a smile. Allie nudged her, just as Thomas and Ryan walked up. "Dr. Shaw, you look beautiful. I think weddings become you," said Ryan.

She swept the bouquet behind her back. "Thank you." She bit her bottom lip.

Thomas took Michelle by the hand and they both took to the dance floor.

Hannah started humming the wedding march.

There was hope and love in the air that day. It was anybody's guess who the next bride from Evergreen would be.

The End

Incredible Apple Dumplings

A Hallmark Original Recipe

In *Christmas In Evergreen: Letters to Santa,* the Chris Kringle Kitchen is where Lisa and Kevin sometimes take a break from fixing up Daisy's General Store. It's also where Michelle first meets Thomas...and where people gossip about romances and other small-town news. One of the specialties at Chris Kringle Kitchen are the famous apple dumplings, which are even more incredible served with a little extra sauce. They're easier than they look, and your friends and family will remember them forever.

Yield: 6 servings
Prep Time: 40 minutes
Cook Time: 60 minutes

INGREDIENTS

Pastry Brisée:

- 3¾ cups all-purpose flour
- 1 tablespoon granulated sugar
- 1 teaspoon kosher salt
- 1½ cups (3 sticks) unsalted butter, cubed
- ¾ cup ice water

Walnut Streusel:

- ½ cup toasted walnuts, chopped
- ¼ cup brown sugar, packed
- 2 tablespoons butter, room temperature
- ¼ teaspoon ground cinnamon
- 1/8 teaspoon ground nutmeg

Brown Sugar Cider Sauce:

- 2 cups brown sugar, packed
- 1¼ cups apple cider
- 1 pinch kosher salt
- ½ teaspoon cinnamon
- 1 teaspoon vanilla extract

Apple Dumplings:

- 6 sweet-tart baking apples (such as Pink Lady or Granny Smith apples)
- 1 egg, beaten

DIRECTIONS

1. To prepare pastry brisée: combine flour, sugar, and salt in bowl of a processor fitted with a steel blade. Pulse to blend. Add cold butter and pulse until mixture resembles coarse corn meal. Slowly add ice water, as needed, to form pastry dough. Divide pastry into 3 equal portions; chill 30 minutes.

2. To prepare walnut streusel: combine walnuts, brown sugar, softened butter, cinnamon, and nutmeg in a small bowl and blend with a fork. Reserve at room temperature.

3. To prepare brown sugar cider sauce: combine brown sugar, apple cider, and salt in a saucepan. Bring to a boil; reduce heat and simmer for 2 minutes. Remove from heat, add cinnamon and vanilla and stir to blend. Reserve.

4. To assemble apple dumplings: using an apple corer or paring knife, core apples and peel. Stuff the center of each apple with walnut streusel filling.

5. Roll out 1 portion of pastry into about an 8-by-16-inch rectangle on a floured work surface; cut into two 7-inch squares. Repeat with remaining pastry dough (to equal six 7-inch squares). Brush outer edges of each pastry square with egg wash. Place 1 apple in the center of each square; bring the corners of

pastry up over the apple to meet in the center and press seams. Cut leaf shapes out of excess pastry if desired, brush with egg wash, and arrange on dumplings. Chill apple dumplings until pastry dough is firm (about 30 minutes, or overnight).

6. Preheat oven to 400°F.

7. Arrange chilled apple dumplings in a large (14-by-11-inch) baking dish. Pour brown sugar cider sauce over dumplings. Bake uncovered for 15 minutes. Reduce oven temperature to 350°F and bake an additional 40 to 45 minutes, or until pastry is golden and apples are just starting to bubble.

8. Serve apple dumpling warm topped with sauce in baking dish. If desired, serve with whipped cream or vanilla ice cream.

9. Baker's tip: place remaining walnut streusel on a small baking sheet lined with baking paper. Heat in a preheated oven at 400°F for 2 to 3 minutes or until butter is melted and bubbly. Cool streusel and serve crumbled over the top of dumplings.

Thanks so much for reading *Christmas in Evergreen: Letters to Santa*. We hope you enjoyed it!

You might like these other books from Hallmark Publishing:

Christmas in Evergreen
The Secret Ingredient
A Down Home Christmas
The Christmas Company
At the Heart of Christmas
A Timeless Christmas

For information about our new releases and exclusive offers, sign up for our free newsletter at hallmarkchannel.com/hallmark-publishing-newsletter

You can also connect with us here:

Facebook.com/HallmarkPublishing

Twitter.com/HallmarkPublish